THE TITANS HEIR

BY
DAFYDD WILLIAMS

This book goes out to my old English teacher for always believing in me.

Table Of Content

My Home 1

My Principle Is A Harpy 5

My Best Friend Is The Daughter Of Zeus 12

Minotaur Of Moonlight Valleys 18

Welcome To The Fortress Of Half-Bloods 24

Message From The Lord Of Thunder 31

Quest Of The Titan's Child 39

The Quest Begins 46

Help From A Distant Traveler 53

Help From The God Of Traveler's 61

Hunted By Powerful Beast 67

Visit From War Itself 73

The Road Trip Plan 84

They Come For Me Again 94

The Goddesses Of Vengeance Attack 102

Saved By A Familiar Friend 110

We Finally Reach Los Angeles 117

The Entrance To The Dark One's Realm 124

Journey Across The Underworld 132

The Betrayal 142

The Tearful Goodbye 156

About The Author 164

References In This Book 165

MY HOME

People always say my name is strange. Back when my life was ordinary before the gods tried to kill me, I heard it all the time. Let me tell you about myself and how I became number one on the Olympians' most-wanted list.

I'm Gwen Sallow, a 12-year-old girl born outside Richmond, Virginia. I have long, golden-blonde hair tied up in a ponytail, ocean-blue eyes that remind people of the sea on a bright, sunny day, and lightly tanned skin like I spent every weekend on vacation. I'm your typical country girl, born and raised in the heart of Virginia, a state filled with rolling hills, valleys, and a rich history. I love every bit of this breathtaking place.

I live on a farm called Moonlight Valleys, named for how the moon's radiant light blankets the land on cloudless nights. I share this home with my mother, Catherine Sallow. She inherited the farm from my grandfather, William Sallow, who passed away five months ago under mysterious circumstances. His death left a hole in my heart he was the closest thing I had to a father. My real dad? Never around. I've never met him, and honestly, I don't care to. My mom still talks about him like he's some misunderstood saint, but I don't understand her sometimes.

My mother and I look so alike that we could be mistaken for sisters except for her light green eyes, which remind me of sunlit meadows. She works tirelessly to keep our farm running while raising me to be strong, independent, and kind. I admire her determination, even though her teasing sometimes gets on my nerves.

Our farm stretches across 444 acres, bordered by thick woods. We raise cows, chickens, sheep, pigs, and two horses: a stallion named Bucephalus, after Alexander the Great's legendary horse, and a mare named Amphitrite, after the mighty sea goddess and wife of Poseidon. Bucephalus is a massive brown Percheron with deep, soulful brown eyes, while Amphitrite is an independent and strong-willed Assateague wild horse with a flowing black mane and tail. My mom found her as a teenager and raised her, joking that it was good training for when I was born. I hated the comparison, but I knew she meant well.

Greek mythology has always fascinated me from the primordial gods to the great Titan Wars and the rule of Zeus. I don't just admire it; I believe in it. I've even converted to Hellenism, though my mom dismisses it as foolish. She says myths shouldn't be taken seriously, unlike Christianity. But belief is personal, and this is mine.

My grandfather built our farmhouse in 1945; it is old but filled with history. A bright green picket fence my grandfather's favourite colour surrounds it, and a small burn mark mars one side, supposedly from a lightning strike decades ago. Inside, the living room holds a large brown couch, an antique lamp in the corner, and a bookshelf filled with my grandfather's favourite novels. A portrait of us together sits atop the fireplace, a constant reminder of what I lost.

Every evening at 6:30 sharp, my mom calls me for dinner she has an uncanny sense of time. Tonight, we eat spaghetti and meatballs. As usual, she asks about school. I tell her it's fine, except for my ADHD and dyslexia making things difficult. She smiles and says, "They're not disabilities but gifts from your gods. Use them." I know she's trying to help, but it feels patronizing, especially since she doesn't believe in Hellenism. Still, I let it go.

After dinner, I treat myself to my favourite dessert a mix of strawberry, vanilla, and chocolate ice cream, which I call the "Sallow Special." Jokingly, I tell myself I could start a company selling it, though I know that's unlikely.

Later, I head upstairs to my bedroom on the third floor, right next to the attic. No one has entered my grandfather's old room since he passed. I get ready for bed and pick up my favourite book series, a Greek mythology-inspired series by R.R. His stories always make me feel connected to the characters as if they were real. I've often wondered what life would be like if I lived in his world.

Little did I know that night would be my last taste of normal life. The next morning, the gods would change everything.

MY PRINCIPLE IS A HARPY

The alarm blared at 8:00 AM, jarring me from sleep. I groaned, burying my face into the pillow. Mornings were the worst. I had always been a night owl, preferring the quiet solitude of the evening. If I were a Demi-God, I'd probably be a daughter of Athena except that was impossible since Athena had sworn an oath on the River Styx to remain a virgin, just like Artemis and Hestia.

Yawning, I pushed myself out of bed and glanced out the window. The golden morning sun bathed the farm in a warm orange glow, illuminating the fields, trees, and distant mountains. It was breathtaking, a sight constantly reminding me of my home's beauty.

After getting dressed for school, I made my way downstairs, where the smell of pancakes and maple syrup greeted me. My mom, as always, had prepared breakfast and packed my lunch a jam sandwich, a packet of crisps, and a carton of apple juice. She did everything for me despite managing the entire farm on her own, a testament to how incredible she was.

"Have a good day, sweetheart," she said as I grabbed my bag.

I sighed at the thought of the two-mile walk to the bus stop. Living on the outskirts of Richmond meant an hour-long commute into the city. Mondays made it worse. They were the absolute worst boring, exhausting, and slow. I put on my headphones, drowning out the silence with my usual rock and musical playlists as I finally made it to the bus stop.

The minibus eventually pulled up; its familiar white exterior lined with small black stripes slowly approaching. We called it the Zebra Bus. It wasn't a regular school bus it was for kids who needed "extra help," though, at my school, that meant "problem kids." I slid into my usual corner seat, perfectly content to be alone, like always.

That is until my friend Luna Williams gets on the bus. Luna was my only real friend; she was the same age as me. We had been inseparable since preschool. She had short, bright blonde hair streaked with purple, though she never bothered to style it. Messy was just her thing. With her bright blue eyes, piercings, and rocker-chic outfits, she looked like she belonged in a band which made sense, considering she played drums and guitar for our school's band. She was the definition of chaos, but she was my chaos.

As usual, she boarded the bus ten minutes after me, panting and sweaty from sprinting to the bus stop. She immediately flopped down next to me, grinning. "Morning, cowgirl."

I rolled my eyes. "Morning, tomboy."

This was our usual banter. Luna teased me about everything from my farm work to my grades and my lack of interest in boys. She had been relentless about that since I found a secret admirer letter in my locker.

"You sure you don't wanna give your mystery Romeo a chance?" she teased.

I groaned. "Drop it, Luna."

She laughed. "You're too easy. You need to get thicker skin, kitten."

Despite her teasing, Luna was fiercely protective of me. If anyone else tried to mess with me, she had no problem throwing punches. Once, she even broke a boy's leg for harassing me and got suspended for two weeks. "No regrets," she had said. "If anyone hurts you, I'll send them straight to Tartarus."

She wasn't joking either. She took my belief in Greek mythology more seriously than I did.

After the boring morning of classes, lunchtime rolled around. Luna and I were enjoying our lunches when Amanda, the resident mean girl, decided to target Luna.

"Tomboy freak," she sneered.

I saw red. Before I could think, I punched her.

As I did everything seemed to slow down. I felt off like the world had shifted in a way I couldn't understand. Then Principle Victoria Locket appeared her short grey hair and her very skinny figure gave off a commanding appearance immediately snapped me out of my trance as she told Amanda and me to follow her.

Now, Luna started to follow, but the principal stopped her. "Not you, Miss Williams. I'll hear your side later."

Luna looked terrified, which terrified me but I nodded to Luna suggesting it will be ok.

I followed Principal Victoria and Amanda toward the gym. It was a cold day, much colder than it had been this morning, which was peculiar. The grey clouds suddenly started to surround the sky, making me uneasy, but nobody else noticed the strange weather patterns around us. Amanda was constantly sorting out her makeup, which usually consisted of expensive foundation, blush, lipstick, and eye shadow. I don't know why a girl her age needs all that makeup; but she needs it for some bizarre reason. And now, she was making sure I "didn't mess up her hair." She was always a cry-baby about everything. She is a spoiled rotten princess, which was probably her parents' fault.

When we arrived at the gym, Principal Victoria and Amanda looked at me like they were going to throw me to a fate worse than death once they were finished with me. As I walked in, the principal locked the door behind us.

"I got you," she whispered. "Turns out Lord Zeus was right."

I blinked. "What?"

Amanda smirked. "Don't play dumb, Half-Blood. You know exactly what you are."

I took a step back. "I have no clue what you're talking about."

Principal Victoria's eyes burned with fury. "You really don't know, do you? You don't even know who your father is."

Something inside me twisted. "My father?"

She sneered. "Doesn't matter. I'll kill you before you realize your true power."

Their bodies began to glow, their forms shifting. Feathers sprouted, wings unfurled, and their arms and legs morphed into those of giant vultures.

Harpies.

"The hounds of Zeus," I breathed.

They lunged at me and time seemed to slow again if only briefly allowing me to just barely dodge the attack. My mind screamed at me to fight back, but how? I had no weapons, no powers, nothing my mind began to race with fear.

Then Luna burst through the doors, her presence commanding attention. It was as if her arrival snapped me back to reality. Her eyes, glowing with a fierce electric blue, locked onto the Harpies. With a voice that carried the fury of an entire army, she bellowed, "Get away from her, in the name of my father Zeus, I command you!"

Her words seemed to shake the air itself. Her eyes burned with a bright white light, tinged with a light blue glow, and bolts of lightning shot from them as if she were made of pure storm energy. The room grew cold, and the wind howled, mirroring the tempest outside.

Could it have been Luna? Was she capable of this? No, it couldn't be; no human could control the weather. Yet, as I stood there, watching the impossible unfold, I couldn't find the words to explain what I witnessed. Her anger flared, growing more intense with every passing moment as she confronted the Harpies.

Lightning sparked in her hands.

I stared in shock. "Luna?"

The Harpies screeched in fury. "Daughter of Zeus
"

Luna didn't let them finish. She hurled a bolt of lightning, instantly reducing them to ashes. The storm dissipated. The room returned to normal as if nothing had happened.

I turned to her, trembling. "Luna... what was that? How did you?"

She grabbed my arm. "No time. You're in danger. We need to get to your mom now."

We ran. Away from the school, away from everything I thought I knew straight into a world I never expected to be part of.

MY BEST FRIEND IS THE DAUGHTER OF ZEUS

We ran out of the gymnasium at full speed, bolting straight for the bus stop about five minutes from the school. We didn't stop or look behind us for even a second. Luna looked pale and terrified. I had so many questions, but she shook her head and whispered every time I tried to ask, "Not now; wait until we're on the bus, and I'll explain everything."

When we reached the bus stop, the bus was nowhere in sight. However, by some stroke of luck, a taxi station was right next to it. Without hesitation, Luna grabbed my arm and practically shoved me into the back seat of a cab. She pulled some spare money from her pocket and handed it to the driver. "Take us to her address," she ordered. I was surprised she even knew where I lived, I was sure I had only told her once or twice, and she only visited every other weekend.

As we drove along the road, past mountains and towering trees, Luna began muttering something under her breath. I barely caught the words: "In the name of the great Goddess Hecate, help me use your power to block all sound around us." A bright green glow surrounded us. "Good," she said, exhaling. "They can't hear us now."

Luna turned to me and saw the terror and confusion in my eyes. "I can finally explain everything," she said, her voice softer now. I was desperate for answers. I had just been attacked by literal Harpies creatures out of Greek mythology. At least, I was pretty sure they were Harpies.

A flood of questions filled my mind. Were they really Harpies? Or was I seeing things? How did everything return to normal after the battle? But one question pressed at me the most. Back there, you shouted something: 'In the name of my father, Zeus, I command you, your human right.' What did you mean by that?"

At first, Luna didn't answer, as if she were searching for the right words that wouldn't make her sound crazy. After a long pause, she finally spoke, her voice uncertain yet determined. "You believe in Hellenism. The Gods of Olympus, right?" I nodded.

"Well," she continued, "those Gods are real. And they have children with mortals. Demigods or as we are more commonly referred to Half-Bloods."

My breath caught in my throat. I had always believed in the Greek Gods, but to hear someone say they were real and to say it with such certainty was something else entirely. It felt like my whole world had just been flipped upside down.

Once I gathered my thoughts, I asked her quietly, "Does that mean... Luna, are you a Half-Blood? Are you the daughter of a God?"

She met my gaze with a stern expression and said, "Yes. I am a Half-Blood, Gwen. I am the daughter of Z " She faltered for a moment before steeling herself. "I am the daughter of Zeus. The King of all the Gods, Ruler of Olympus. That's how I summon lightning and change the weather."

I stared at her in shock. "You're the daughter of Zeus? Like, *the* Zeus son of Cronus, God of Lightning and the Sky?" My best friend the girl I had known since preschool was the daughter of a literal God. It was almost too much to take in. But one question nagged at me. "Why would Zeus' daughter be hanging out with nobody like me? My family has only ever been farmers."

Luna's expression softened. "You're far from a 'nobody,' Gwen. Chiron knew that from the day you were born. That's why he made me your Keeper."

"Keeper?" I repeated, frowning. "And wait Chiron? As in the centaur, the trainer of heroes?"

Luna nodded, "a Keeper is a Half-Blood who already knows their divine parent and is trained to use their abilities. They're assigned to protect another Half-Blood until they're ready to learn the truth about their heritage. This usually happens around the ages of twelve or thirteen."

This was too much. My head spun. "But why would I need a Keeper? I'm not a Half-Blood. I'm completely human." Luna let out a short laugh. "Oh, Gwen, you are *not* fully human. You're like me you're a Half-Blood. And a mighty one at that." She leaned forward. "Don't you remember slowing down time earlier? When you pushed Amanda or again just briefly before I arrived to dodge the Harpies attack even if it was accidental. If that wasn't a sign, I don't know what is."

I blinked. "You noticed that? I thought I was imagining things adrenaline or something."

Luna smiled. "Of course I noticed. Half-Bloods recognize each other's powers. And let me tell you I've seen a lot of demigods, but you shocked even me with how strong you were. Just like Chiron always expected."

I took a shaky breath. If what she and Chiron believed was true, then I wasn't just a Half-Blood I was the descendant of a mighty God. But something about the way Luna spoke of Chiron caught my attention it was like She admired him, and you could hear that admiration in her voice it was almost like in her eyes he could do no wrong so. I decided to ask, "What's Chiron like?"

She hesitated before answering. "Chiron raised me," she admitted. "My mother... she gave me away when I was just a baby. She didn't want to raise a Half-Blood." Her voice was steady, but I could hear the pain beneath it. "Chiron is a great teacher. A father figure. He has a black horse's lower body and a man's upper body. He wears a black suit, a neatly trimmed black beard, and matching hair. His eyes are light blue. He's wise, patient, and strong."

I had always known Luna had issues with her mother, but now I truly understood why. She had been abandoned left behind simply because of who she was. My heart ached for her.

But then another thought struck me. "Luna... you're the daughter of Zeus."

"Correct," she said.

"And those creatures that attacked us were Harpies."

"Also correct."

"Harpies are known as the 'guard dogs' of Zeus." I swallowed hard. "Which means *your father* sent them after me. Why would Zeus want to hurt me?"

Luna's jaw tightened. "I don't know," she admitted. "But I swear, Gwen, I will find out. And I will protect you. No matter what."

As we neared my farm, the sky darkened. The storm clouds were back. "Is this you?" I asked Luna.

She shook her head. "No. I think my father might be angry at me for helping you."

The taxi pulled up to the entrance, and the driver warned us to be careful. As we stepped out, a bone-chilling roar echoed through the woods surrounding the farm. My blood ran cold. Whatever made that sound... it was coming for us.

MINOTAUR OF MOONLIGHT VALLEYS

The roar echoed through the valley, freezing me in place. My mind raced with possibilities of what could have made such a sound.

Luna grabbed my arm, her fingers digging into my flesh. "We need to head for the house now!"

We sprinted up the rugged dirt path, stones skittering beneath our feet. The front door crashed open under our weight, bringing Mom running from downstairs.

"What in heaven's name is going on?" she demanded. "Why are you girls back so early? And for the love of God, stop trying to break down the door! Do you want all of Richmond to hear you?" Her eyes settled on Luna, confusion creasing her features.

Luna's voice trembled. "She's been discovered. I tried to keep her hidden, but now we have to go." The words seemed to pain her physically.

"No." Mom's voice cracked with fear. "There must be another way. I can't lose my daughter. Luna, you promised you'd do anything to help us avoid this fate!"

Luna bowed her head, tears glinting in her eyes. "I'm so sorry, Miss Sallow. Truly. You're a good mother, and you've always done your best for her, but Gwen isn't safe here anymore. It's not just monsters now the Gods themselves are involved. She must come with me, for her own protection. Please, for Gwen's sake."

Mom's shoulders slumped in defeat. "If Gwen is in that much danger... then I must set my feelings aside for her safety."

A massive crash shook the front gate, followed by another roar louder and more savage than before. The sound penetrated to my very soul, leaving me paralyzed with terror. We rushed to the window, and my blood turned to ice.

The creature stood seven feet tall, its torso resembling a massive bodybuilder. But where a human head should have been, dark horns curved from a bovine skull. Black fur covered its legs, and its red eyes blazed with hatred. A long tail lashed behind it.

"MINOTAUR!" Luna's scream broke the spell of horror. She froze for a moment before whispering, "We need to run. Is there anywhere we can go?"

Mom hesitated, then admitted, "The only way out is through that front gate."

Luna's face fell, but she quickly turned to the sink. Speaking another spell, she tossed a drachma into the water. "Oh radiant lady Iris, accept my offering."

The water glowed with rainbow colors, responding, "Offering accepted."

Luna spoke rapidly into the prismatic mist: "Send a message to Chiron at to frourio than emiaemun." Surprisingly, I understood the Greek phrase "the fortress of Half-bloods." Whether this ability to understand Greek came from being a Half-blood, I couldn't say, but the words made perfect sense to me.

"Chiron, Gwen has been discovered, but we're trapped on her farm by the Minotaur," Luna continued. "We need help. I'll hold out as long as I can, but send help I can't hold it back forever." The rainbow dissipated.

Luna turned to us, her expression grim. "I'll hold off the Minotaur. You two need to hide."

"No!" I protested. "I'm a half-blood too. I can help fight!"

"You don't know how to control your powers," Luna countered. "The monster wants you. I can fight better just stay hidden, Gwen. Promise me."

I nodded reluctantly. Luna managed a smile before stepping outside. Her eyes blazed with brilliant blue light as sparks began to dance around them.

The Minotaur roared in challenge, fixing its rage-filled gaze on Luna as Mom and I ducked into the closet. Thunder crashed outside, each boom shaking the house to its foundation. I couldn't stay hidden while Luna risked her life. Despite Mom's desperate pleas, I burst from our hiding place.

The house lay in ruins. Family portraits shattered on the floor, furniture splintered, and our animals including my beloved horses had fled in terror. Luna hurled thunderbolt after thunderbolt, but each attack only seemed to enrage the monster further. Finally, the Minotaur's massive hand closed around her. Luna's cry of pain cut through me as the beast hurled her against the last standing wall.

"Gwen... please... run..." Luna's words faded as she lost consciousness.

"LUNA!" My scream drew the Minotaur's attention. Fear and rage warred in my chest as I shouted, "It's me you want? Then come get me!"

I ran, the monster's thundering footsteps close behind. Its grip closed around me, and I screamed in agony. "Let go of me, you filthy monster!"

Suddenly, an orange glow enveloped me. Time seemed to slow once again, allowing me to slip from the Minotaur's grasp. One of Luna's fallen thunderbolts lay nearby. When I grabbed it, searing pain shot through my arm like thousands of white-hot needles piercing my flesh. The agony intensified until my entire arm felt like it was dissolving in fire, but I forced myself to focus on one thought: protecting Mom and Luna.

With everything I had, I hurled the bolt. It struck true, piercing the Minotaur's heart and reducing the monster to ash.

The world spun around me. I staggered back toward the house, finding Luna still unconscious but breathing. "Mom?" I called weakly, but no answer came. The lightning had taken its toll my head felt light, and nausea gripped my stomach. My knees buckled, and as my vision darkened, I glimpsed two figures approaching a tall man who seemed to be part horse and a young boy beside him I think he looked a year older than Luna and me.

"How did she manage to grab one of Luna's lightning bolts?" the boy asked. "There's no way she's another child of Zeus look at the white scars on her arm."

The man's voice was grave. "No, I do not believe she is a child of Zeus. However, this girl is incredibly Powerful. We must take them to the fortress that's all we can do for them both right now."

As consciousness slipped away, questions swirled in my mind: Who were these strangers? What did they want? And what did they mean about my power? I didn't feel powerful just terrified and useless, like I couldn't do anything to protect those I loved. Whatever was happening, I knew my life would never be the same after what had transpired in the Moonlight Valleys.

WELCOME TO THE FORTRESS OF HALF-BLOODS

I don't know how long it had been since encountering the Minotaur. My memories were scattered, slipping in and out of consciousness. Voices echoed around me, fragmented and distant.

The first time I woke, I heard Luna's voice. She sounded distraught.

"I'm so sorry, Chiron. I failed as a keeper. I failed to defeat the Minotaur and keep her safe. Look at her left arm the scars from when she grabbed my lightning bolt. She's lucky to be alive... no thanks to me."

A deep, calm voice responded. I recognised it the same one I had heard before losing consciousness at the farm.

"No, child, it was my fault. I should have known that someone as powerful as her would attract more than just the usual monsters. I should have been more careful when assigning you this task. But even Zeus wants her dead... I wonder why. We must tread carefully with this information, Luna."

"I agree," Luna said solemnly.

Darkness swallowed me once again.

The second time I surfaced, I heard Luna talking to someone else a boy, I recognised his voice it was the same one from the farm.

"Luna, this girl has to be someone powerful. She grabbed one of your lightning bolts, and she's not even a child of Zeus! Look at her arm the scars, the white lightning marks... I don't know what kind of Half-Blood you brought back, but she must be powerful to survive touching Zeus's lightning."

Luna sighed. "You think I don't know that, Peter? I've been friends with her since preschool, and now I learn my father wants one of my best friends dead. And nobody knows why."

Peter was quiet for a moment before replying, his tone skeptical. "She's safe here... for now."

Their voices faded as I slipped under again.

When I woke for the third time, I managed to keep my eyes open. The world around me came into focus sort of.

I was in a room that looked like a hospital ward, but something was off. The walls were green, the air smelled like damp earth, and the nurses if they could even be called that weren't human. They had green skin and long, vine-like hair and moved with an unnatural grace.

I blinked, trying to process everything. I glanced down at my left arm and froze. White lightning scars wrapped around it like jagged tattoos. So that's what they meant when they said look what happened when I grabbed the lightning bolt...

"Tree nymphs," a familiar voice said beside me.

I turned to see Luna standing there, her expression a mix of relief and amusement. "They're tree nymphs, Gwen. Usually, the children of Apollo act as our doctors, but they were all busy. You gave me a scare. Please don't ever do that again."

Despite everything, I managed a weak smile. "I'll try."

"What happened with the Minotaur?" I asked.

"Destroyed," Luna said. "Thanks to you. Not a lot of people can grab my lightning bolts. That power usually belongs to Zeus's children. Can you imagine if we're secretly siblings? But I doubt it." She smirked. "I'm sorry about your arm, though. Hey, at least you have some battle scars now, right?"

I laughed. It felt nice having her here.

"How did we get out of the farm?" I asked after a moment.

"Chiron came with Peter. He's a son of Athena. They carried us back to the fortress. You've been unconscious for about six weeks. I barely left your side."

Six weeks? My mind reeled. That opened up many more questions, but one hit me harder than the rest.

"My mom what happened to my mom?" I asked, my voice urgent.

Luna's face fell. She hesitated before saying, "We... don't know. She disappeared. No trace, no sign of where she went."

I stared at her, my mind racing. My mother gone? How? The last time I saw her; she was in the closet... hiding from the minotaur. Had she been taken? Had I left her to die? The thought made me feel physically ill.

Luna placed a hand on my shoulder. "We'll find her, Gwen."

I barely registered her words.

A few minutes later, after gathering myself, Luna handed me a set of clothes. "Get changed and meet me outside. I'll show you around."

I looked at the uniform. It consisted of light blue trousers and a white shirt with the words *"Half-Blood Fortress"* printed across it, with a small image of a fortress in the center.

When I stepped outside, Luna smiled. "Nice fit. Come on, let's go."

As we walked along a forest path, she pointed things out. "To the right is the archery range and the stables. Mostly children of Ares and Apollo train here."

I watched kids practice with swords, rode horses, and fired arrows at targets with surprising accuracy.

Further along, Luna gestured to a massive building. "This is the mess hall. All of us gather here at meal times. Different cabins, different gods, but we all eat together."

We turned a corner, and I saw cabins scattered across the hills. Each one was unique. "Those are the different god cabins," Luna explained. "Ares' cabin is bright red, covered in skulls and weapons. Athena's cabin is lined with silver and decorated with owl symbols."

"Which one's yours?" I asked.

She grinned. "Follow me."

We climbed a steep hill until we reached three cabins.

Luna pointed at a black one adorned with statues of three-headed dogs. "Hades' cabin." Then she gestured to a deep blue one with fishing nets and a trident symbol. "Poseidon's." Finally, she turned to the center a light blue cabin streaked with gold thunderbolts and eagles. "And that's mine. The only child of the Big Three up here, so I get the best view."

I laughed. "Of course you do."

A voice called from behind us. "Luna."

Luna turned, and her face lit up. "Chiron!"

I followed her gaze and froze. Standing there was a centaur exactly as Luna had described him. The lower half was a sleek black horse, while the upper half looked like an Oxford professor, complete with a tweed jacket.

He studied me with knowing eyes. "So, you're showing Gwen around? Good. Nice to see you again, Gwen."

I frowned. "Again?"

Chiron chuckled. "Yes, child. The last time I saw you, you were six months old. We've been waiting for your arrival for a long time."

I swallowed hard. "Why?"

"That," he said with a cryptic smile, "is something we'll discuss soon. For now, let's get you settled."

He turned to Luna. "Take her to the Hermes cabin. Explain the situation."

Luna nodded. We walked to a cabin that looked... well, rough. It was cluttered with travel bags and old statues of Hermes. Luna sighed. "Hermes is the god of travelers. So, until your godly parent claims you, this is where you stay."

She set me up with a bunk and promised to see me at dinner.

And then she was gone.

I understood she had to leave for now but in that moment I had never felt more alone in a room full of people.

MESSAGE FROM THE LORD OF THUNDER

Dinnertime arrived, just like every other evening, around 6:00 PM. I followed the Hermes cabin into the dining hall, where everyone took their usual places. First came Luna from the Zeus cabin, followed by the other children of the main gods. Luna was the only one from the children of the big three gods so she walked in alone. Then, a boy who was with the Athena cabin walked in. One kid shouted, "Hey Peter!" so I knew this was Peter, the son of Athena. He had pale white skin, short brown hair, and grey cloudy eyes.

The other Olympian cabins followed, each one in order, with respect to the gods they descended from. I sat down at the Hermes table and asked one of the boys, "Why do we all follow this order?" He turned to me, smiled, and said, "It's a sign of respect. We keep to the order of our godly parents and their power in the world. No mixing."

Chiron, perched on a pillar, rose to make a speech. "Thank you all for an amazing day. We give thanks to the Mighty Gods and Goddesses of Olympus and to the arrival of our new powerful ally. I am, of course, talking about Miss Sallow."

Everyone's attention shifted toward me, and I felt uncomfortable under their gaze. Chiron seemed to notice and quickly changed the subject.

"Anyway," he continued, "let the feast commence!" With a snap of his fingers, a spread of food appeared on the table: pork, steak, fish, vegetables, and every drink imaginable. Some of the cabin members began pouring food into the fire, and I turned to the boy beside me again, asking, "Why is everyone pouring food into the fire?"

He replied, "It's an offering to the gods. It's not enough that we're their kids and they rule the universe. They like to feel appreciated, so we sacrifice food to please them."

I grabbed some chicken with potatoes and made my offering to the gods as a sign of respect. As I ate, I glanced across the room and noticed Chiron, Luna, and Peter all staring at me from their tables. I couldn't help but wonder why they were looking at me.

Then I received a message on my phone from Luna. It read: "Meet me by the campfire after food. I'll introduce you to Peter. You'll like him. Trust me, he's been my friend for almost as long as you."

After dinner, I found Luna sitting next to Peter on a log by the campfire. Hesitant at first, I finally walked over and sat next to her. She smiled and officially introduced me.

"Peter, this is Gwen Sallow. Gwen, this is Peter Winter."

"Nice to meet you at last," Peter said, grinning. "Luna's told me a lot about you. It's so nice to finally meet you. Let me tell you about myself. I'm thirteen years old, and I've been here since birth, same as Luna. I'm the son of Athena and also the head of the Athena cabin, since I've been here the longest."

"Hi," I said shyly. "I'm Gwen. I grew up on a farm my whole life, believing in Greek mythology. Still shocked that I was right. Apparently, I'm the child of someone powerful, though I don't know who. Also, a Minotaur tried to kill me."

Peter grinned, though his smile held a certain understanding. "Don't worry. We'll figure it out. A lot of half-bloods don't know their godly parent. Most gods don't really care unless you're a full god or there's a super-secret prophecy about you."

"PETER!" Luna shouted suddenly.

Peter immediately went quiet. "Sorry," he muttered. "But I do hope we can be friends. Luna's always talked about you during your summer holidays. I think we'll get along great."

I smiled. "Sure, you seem like a nice guy. It'll be nice to have another friend here."

At that, Luna and Peter burst out laughing. Luna wiped a tear from her eye and said, still chuckling, "See, Peter? I told you. She's socially awkward."

I blushed, feeling a little embarrassed. But, well, it was Luna. I knew how she could be.

Two weeks passed quickly. I spent almost every day with Peter, reading books; mainly fiction and fantasy. It was nice to have another bookworm to talk to. Luna tried to get me into sword training, but I wasn't very good. I kept losing my balance and falling, which earned me some laughs from the children of Ares. Luna reassured me, "We just haven't found the right weapon for you yet. And this training will help you. Monsters outside the barrier will never stop hunting you. This place is protected by Hecate's magic, under the orders of Zeus."

It was strange to learn the camp was protected by Hecate's magic. As for weapons, nothing seemed to work for me. I tried archery and almost shot Peter's head off. He wasn't bothered, though; he laughed for a good ten minutes. I tried everything: swordplay, magic, archery. But nothing seemed to click—until one day.

I was training with Peter when he nearly caught me off guard, which made sense since his mother was the Goddess of Battle Strategy. However, everything suddenly slowed down again as I was thrown to the floor. Time seemed to slow to a crawl, so I grabbed my wooden sword and swung it at him, hitting him across the face.

When the time returned to normal, Peter was on the ground, screaming. "I... I... I'm so sorry, Peter!" I said, rushing to him.

Peter, still laughing, shook his head. "Sorry? Why in the name of Zeus are you sorry? That was amazing! What was that? You slowed down time with an orange glow, and I've never seen a power like that before. It's not associated with any god that I know of."

My face turned red. "I don't know how I do it. My powers just happen randomly, and I don't have much control over them."

Peter smiled. "Well, however you did it, that was amazing! I'll help you control it. Me and Luna will both help. But I have no idea which god has your powers."

"Thanks," I said gratefully.

Dinner came around again at 6:00. As usual, Chiron made his speech before snapping his fingers, and the food appeared. I grabbed some pork chops with a handful of vegetables, made my offering to the gods, and then went to join Luna and Peter by the campfire outside the dining hall.

We spent some time casually chatting about how our days had gone, how my training was progressing, and, of course, about my strange powers. Peter was still curious, but then something strange happened.

The fire suddenly turned blue, and a storm of lightning surrounded it. From the fire emerged the king of the gods himself, Zeus.

"Zeus!" Chiron cried. "What is the meaning of this? You know this place is a sanctuary for demigods only!"

Zeus looked far more terrifying in person. He had black hair, piercing light blue eyes, dark blue lightning bolts crackling from them. His skin was tanned, and he wore a light blue suit that didn't seem to be damaged by the storm he was creating.

Zeus glared down at Chiron. "You lost that privilege when you decided to harbor a fugitive that I tried to kill. I would've succeeded if my daughter had not shown mercy and interfered in the affairs of the gods."

"Father," Luna cried, her voice trembling. "Why do you want to hurt Gwen? She's a half-blood like me. She hasn't done anything wrong. She hasn't harmed Olympus or the gods."

"Not yet," Zeus sneered. "I'll tell you why I want her dead. It's because of who her father is. It's because of what she will do. An oracle warned me about her."

Luna stepped forward, her voice shaking. "What do you mean? Her father? Who is her godly parent? What do you mean by 'what she'll do?'"

Zeus' anger flared. "You seriously have no idea, stupid girl? She is my half-sister. Her father is Cronus, the Titan Lord, God of Time and the Harvest."

I froze, my heart pounding in my chest. Cronus? That was impossible. He was locked in Tartarus after the war between the Titans and the gods.

"That's impossible!" Luna cried. "Father, you must have made a mistake!"

With a clap of thunder, Zeus' voice boomed, "SILENCE! I make no mistakes. My daughter, you will be wise to remember your place. Hear my words, Gwen Sallow. I have your mother imprisoned in the Castle of Hades. I will release her, but you must go to the Underworld and give yourself in her place. If you do not surrender to Olympus, I will kill your mother, and then I will come for you. You have two weeks. Don't cross me."

With another thunderous clap, Zeus was gone.

I stood there in shock, pale and shaking. "What's going on?" I asked Luna, my voice barely above a whisper.

Everyone stared at me with fear, suspicion, and uncertainty, as though I had suddenly become one of the monsters. Chiron spoke up, breaking the silence.

"Gwen, follow me to the head office. Peter, Luna, you too. Come with me."

We rushed to the head office, and I couldn't shake the horror of what Zeus had just said. Daughter of Cronus? That should be impossible. What did I do now?

QUEST OF THE TITAN'S CHILD

When we entered the head office, Chiron locked the door behind us. Once we knew we were alone, I collapsed on the floor, still terrified, pondering everything I'd just been told. Peter broke the silence first, shouting, "This is impossible, right, Chiron? There's no way for Cronus and his Titans to leave Tartarus! How could he have had a Half-Blood kid? It doesn't make any sense! Luna, did you even know she was the daughter of a Titan?"

Luna shook her head. "Of course I didn't know! How could I have guessed? Her ability to slow time was creepy, but I never suspected this."

"Enough!" Chiron's voice was firm. "You're frightening Gwen. This isn't helping her."

I looked up at Peter and Luna, and for the first time, I saw fear and skepticism in their eyes. I never expected that, not from Luna, especially not after everything we had been through. I gathered myself and spoke, my voice shaky, "I don't understand what's going on any more than you do. I don't know about this prophecy he spoke of. Luna, please, believe me, I would never do anything to hurt you or anyone here."

Luna glanced down, her voice quiet. "Of course we know that. It's just... shocking. We didn't think it was even possible for Cronus to leave Tartarus, let alone have a child with a mortal woman."

Chiron spoke up, his tone grave. "This is a shock to everyone, Gwen. Nobody here believes you would cause harm on purpose. But the daughter of Cronus? That's not a common occurrence. I know the prophecy Zeus is so terrified of. It doesn't end well for the Gods of Olympus, and that's probably why he's so frightened."

Peter's face tightened. "Chiron, if you know the prophecy, can you tell us? Maybe, as the son of Athena, I can help shed some light on this. Maybe I can help Gwen and her mom, who Hades has locked up in the Underworld, by the way."

"I..." Chiron hesitated, his voice faltering. "I can't. I swore an oath on the River Styx never to speak of the prophecy to anyone outside of the main Kings."

"Chiron..." Luna's voice trailed off in disbelief. "Why would you make an oath like that?"

Chiron sighed, looking older than I had ever seen him. "I had no choice. Zeus threatened to throw me in Tartarus and destroy everything I loved if I didn't swear to keep it a secret."

Peter frowned, clearly frustrated. "Okay, then what do we do now? Gwen's mom is locked up in Hades' Castle. The Gods are against us, and they want Gwen captured, maybe even killed. We've got two weeks to figure this out."

I exploded. "What are you suggesting, Peter? That I just let my mother die in the Underworld to save myself? How dare you!"

Chiron intervened before Peter could respond. "Gwen, please calm down. Peter didn't mean it that way. Of course, we would never leave your mother to die in the Underworld. But we have to think realistically. We can't just hand you over either. We have to prove that you won't fulfill the prophecy, and that's easier said than done. We need a strategic plan if we are to succeed. Please, take it easy and calm yourself."

The last part of Chiron's statement stung. "Calm myself? My mother is in a prison in the Underworld, and I've just found out I'm the daughter of a Titan! The Gods want me dead, and there's some secret prophecy about a child of the Titans that's causing all of this. So don't tell me to calm down!"

"Gwen!" Luna shouted. "Chiron is only trying to."

"No," Chiron interrupted. "Do not blame her. I understand her anger more than you realize. After all, I'm also a child of Cronus."

The words hit me hard. I hadn't realized how unfair I'd been. I looked up at Chiron, Luna, and Peter, my voice trembling. "I'm so sorry. I don't know what came over me. All of this... It's just a lot to process. I'm not sure what to do or even what to say in this situation."

Chiron nodded understandingly. "There's no need to apologize, Gwen. In fact, I think it's best if you consult with the Oracle for advice. The Oracle will give you a prophecy, and that will guide our next move."

"Oracle?" I asked, confused.

Chiron's voice was steady. "Yes. There are many Oracles scattered around the world, but we have our own Oracle here at the Fortress. We use it for quests when Half-Bloods need guidance. Go to the basement and speak with the Oracle."

I nodded, unsure of what to expect, and followed Chiron's instructions down the mossy stone steps. The air thickened the farther I went down, until I reached a room made entirely of moss-covered stone. In the center stood a green spirit-like woman, her eyes glowing with emerald lightning. The sight was hypnotizing.

"O great Oracle," I said, my voice unsteady, "I have come seeking your guidance. What will happen if I go to rescue my mother? Give me advice."

The Oracle's eyes flared brighter, and in a rasping voice, she spoke:

> *You shall go West and find the doors to the Dark One's realm.*
> *You shall find your mother and see her safely returned to the overworld.*
> *You shall be looked at with fear and suspicion by those you love and cherish the most.*
> *And find yourself lost and alone when your story is complete.*

The Oracle's words echoed in my mind as her form dissolved into thin air. Stunned, I processed the prophecy. "Lost and alone..." What did that even mean? I pushed it aside. I had to free my mother. That was my focus.

I returned to Chiron and the others, who were waiting for me.

"Well?" Peter asked, leaning forward. "What did the Oracle say?"

I hesitated before speaking. "She said, 'You shall go West and find the doors to the Dark One's realm. You shall find your mother and see her safely returned to the overworld.'"

Luna's face lit up with hope. "That's great news, Gwen!"

"WAIT," Chiron said, cutting through the optimism. "Is that all?"

I played dumb. "Yes, of course."

Chiron studied me, clearly unconvinced. "Remember, Gwen, prophecies can be tricky. Sometimes you won't understand what they mean until they happen."

"Okay, Chiron," I said, nodding slowly. "I'll keep that in mind."

Peter spoke up, breaking the silence. "Well, we know we need to go West. But how exactly do we get to the Underworld?" "we" I asked confused

Luna cut in, her tone firm. "Do you really think I'm going to let my best friend go on a dangerous quest alone? You must have lost your mind if you think I'm not going with you, Gwen. You're stuck with me now, and forever."

Chiron smiled. "To answer your question, Peter, the Underworld is located in Los Angeles, California.

You'll need to find a hotel called The Palace of Death. There, you'll find Charon, the ferryman. Pay him some drachmas, and he'll take you across the River Styx and towards the Underworld's doors."

"Great," Luna said. "But how do we get Gwen's mom out without them taking Gwen?"

Chiron's face grew somber. "That, I don't know. You'll have to figure that out while you travel. I won't lie to you there will be many challenges ahead. The Underworld is dangerous, and very few have made it out alive. Are you still willing to go?"

We all looked at each other, and without hesitation, we nodded in agreement.

"Very well," Chiron said, his voice steady. "If that's the case, I hereby grant permission for this quest to go ahead. You'll leave in the morning. For now, get some rest."

We all nodded and headed to our rooms, the weight of the quest ahead settling over us. Tomorrow, the journey would begin.

THE QUEST BEGINS

We woke up around 8:00 AM, the morning air crisp with anticipation. Chiron had already packed our bags one for each of us filled with food, a travel map, Ambrosia medicine, two hundred dollars, one hundred golden drachmas, spare clothes, and a necklace in my bag alone. Chiron only said when I asked about it, "It will come in handy for the long journey ahead." I didn't understand its purpose, but there was no time to dwell on it.

With Chiron leading us, we made our way toward the fortress border, hidden within the dense forest. You'd never guess a fortress lay beyond the towering trees if you didn't know better. As we reached the edge, we turned back to Chiron. Luna and Peter hugged him goodbye, and I thanked him for everything. He gave me a knowing smile. "No need to thank me, child. Protecting Half-Bloods is my duty I've been doing it for centuries. But I must warn you again, Gwen. You are in incredible danger. Being the daughter of Cronus makes you a threat in many eyes. Stay vigilant."

"I will," I promised, though uncertainty churned inside me.

With that, we stepped into the unknown, a world teeming with monsters and uncertainty.

After descending the mountain, we reached a bus stop on a deserted road. Peter pointed to it, saying, "We should wait here, take the bus west to the furthest town, and then figure things out from there."

Luna shook her head. "That'll take too long. We have only two weeks. We need to move faster."

Peter sighed, frustration flickering across his face. "Think logically, Luna. If we walk, it'll take even longer. The bus gives us time to plan instead of rushing off without a strategy."

Luna crossed her arms. "Oh really? At least my plan involves doing something instead of sitting around."

Tension crackled between them. I exhaled sharply. "This isn't helping. You both have a point, but let's be real we don't know the way to California. The bus is our best bet. At least while we're on it, we can devise a solid plan."

Reluctantly, Luna nodded. We waited.

Thirty minutes later, a long yellow bus with black and red stripes pulled up. We paid ten dollars to the driver and took seats at the back. As the bus rumbled along, silence stretched between us. Finally, Luna spoke, her voice quieter now. "I'm sorry, Peter. I didn't mean to argue. I'm just stressed. The gods themselves are against us. My own father is against us. And they want my best friend dead. I don't know what to do. We don't even know what happens when we reach our destination. We can't just hand Gwen over."

Peter lowered his gaze. "I'm sorry too, Luna. We'll figure something out. Half-Bloods have been in worse situations. We always find a way."

Just then, the bus stopped. The doors creaked open, and my stomach twisted into knots.

Victoria Locket and Amanda stepped inside.

They slid into the seats right in front of us. My breath hitched. How were they alive? Luna struck them with her thunderbolt, hadn't she? Victoria turned; her voice as venomous as ever. "Surprised to see us, little one? You look shocked. Understandable. We're immortal beings. We don't die we disintegrate and respawn in Tartarus or Mount Olympus, depending on who we serve."

My hands clenched. They looked untouched as if they had never been harmed. Victoria smirked. "I take it you've learned who you are Cronus' daughter. Then you must understand why we have to lock you in Tartarus. We must stop the prophecy."

I met her gaze, anger simmering beneath my skin. "I don't even know the prophecy. I just want my mother back."

Amanda sneered. "It doesn't matter what you say. You will bring destruction. Surrender to Lord Hades."

I lifted my chin. "I won't surrender, and I won't be thrown into Tartarus."

Victoria laughed coldly. "I was hoping you'd say that."

In a flash, she slashed at the steering wheel with her claws. The bus swerved. Screams filled the air as we crashed.

A sharp voice dragged me back to consciousness. "We have to get out now!" Peter's urgency snapped me into action.

Luna, Peter, and I shattered the window and climbed out of the wreckage. But Victoria and Amanda were already waiting for us.

Luna summoned a lightning bolt. Peter uncapped his pen, revealing a massive spear etched with ancient Greek symbols. My heart pounded as I reached into my bag. The necklace pulsed, glowing as I touched it. The moment my fingers closed around it, it transformed into a bronze sickle with a black leather grip, its blade lined with silver harvest patterns and jagged spikes.

Victoria smirked. "A sickle? How fitting. Like father, like daughter."

Victoria and Amanda morphed into their Harpy forms in a blinding light, their claws sharpening with a menacing screech.

They attacked in a flurry of motion diving, swooping, too fast to track. Luna summoned a gust of wind, which did little to slow them. She hurled a thunderbolt miss. Amanda cackled. "What's wrong, daughter of Zeus? Losing your touch? Your father must be so disappointed."

Luna's jaw clenched. Peter tried to strategise, but Victoria kept throwing him off-balance. Then, the Harpies unleashed a windstorm in a synchronised flap, knocking us backwards into the wrecked bus.

Pain flared in my ribs. We were trapped.

A surge of frustration boiled inside me. Heat pulsed in my veins. My vision blurred, and suddenly, everything stopped.

The Harpies froze in midair.

Luna gasped. "Gwen... you stopped time."

I blinked. My body felt electric, humming with power. "I guess I did. Cronus is the god of time. So this is one of his abilities."

Peter's voice was wary. "Then this is our chance. Take them down."

I gripped the sickle and swung. A bright orange arc sliced through the frozen Harpies, and they disintegrated into nothing in a blink.

For a moment, we stood in stunned silence.

Luna exhaled. "Gwen... you saved us. But be careful. Cronus' power is dangerous. The gods already fear you. The stronger you get, the more they'll see you as a threat."

My anger flared. "I just saved us, Luna. I can't change who I am. I used my power to help, and you're already doubting me?"

Peter stepped in, his voice gentle. "We're grateful, Gwen. You know that. But the gods won't see it the way we do. We... don't want them to turn against you even more."

I hesitated. Maybe Luna wasn't doubting me just warning me. But for the first time, resentment prickled between us.

"You're right," I murmured. "I'm sorry. It's just... hard."

Luna's expression softened. "Gwen, you're my best friend. We grew up together. You're not like Cronus just like I'm not like Zeus. I never meant to make you feel otherwise."

I swallowed wondering. Should I tell them about the other half of the prophecy? The part that made my blood run cold? No. Not yet.

Instead, I forced a small smile. "Thanks for saying that, Luna." My Sickle turned back into the neckless and I placed it around my neck so I'd always have it on me "Let's keep moving."

We walked for thirty more minutes until we spotted a small hamlet. Relief settled over us.

Luna pointed. "We can rest there and stock up."

Exhausted, starving, and still reeling from the fight, we agreed. Let's hope, the gods will grant us a moment of peace for once.

HELP FROM A DISTANT TRAVELER

We reached the hamlet, but something felt off. The streets were nearly empty, and the few people we saw glanced at us with confusion. Peter shrugged.

"Just ignore them. They probably don't get many visitors. We're the outsiders, and if we want to stay here, we're better off keeping to ourselves."

I frowned. "How do you know that?"

Peter smirked. "Do you know how many small communities exist in my home state of Alaska?"

"No," I admitted.

"One hundred sixty-two," he said with a proud grin.

Luna raised an eyebrow. "Wow, Peter, really?"

"Yup. Not a lot of people know that about my home," he said, his pride evident. Like me, he took great pride in where he came from.

We continued down the stone path until we reached a small inn named *The Traveler's Inn*. The two-story stone building featured medieval-style windows and intricate designs along the walls. At the center, an old black wooden door stood ominously. Peter stopped, his expression shifting.

"That's strange," he muttered.

Luna tilted her head. "What's strange, Peter?"

He gestured toward the door. "It's made from dark oak. That's... no, that's extremely suspicious."

I crossed my arms. "Why? Is there some medieval superstition about dark oak?"

Peter smirked. "Let me explain, Gwen. In medieval times, people didn't usually use dark oak. They relied on the more durable common oak. Seeing a dark wood door on a medieval-style building? That's incredibly unusual."

I shouldn't have been surprised. Peter was the son of Athena, after all.

Luna sighed. "Look, strange door or not, we need a place to rest. We can't stay long, but a day or two will give us time to get our bearings and come up with a plan."

We agreed and approached the wooden door. Peter knocked three times. No answer. Luna rolled her eyes, shoved him aside, and banged on the door four times. It creaked open on its own.

Inside, the dim room flickered with candlelight, the wax flames dancing in eerie synchrony. A short red carpet led to a small, empty reception desk. The oak-wood counter held a ledger, a small wooden chair, and a silver bell in the center.

Peter tensed. "I don't like this. This is setting off all kinds of red flags."

Luna smirked. "Oh, Peter, Gwen must be right. You *are* superstitious. We don't have a choice, though."

She rang the bell three times a soft voice, warm yet aged, called from the back. Moments later, an elderly woman stepped forward. She had long white hair, light brown skin, and wrinkles, befitting her years. She smiled kindly.

"Hello, little ones. My name is Mrs. Jones, but you can call me Carol. This is a small town, and I've never seen you before. What brings you here?"

Luna returned the smile. "Nice to meet you, Carol. We're not from around here. I'm Luna. To my left is Peter, and to my right is Gwen."

Carol studied us before nodding. "Just you three, all alone? Are you looking for a place to stay?"

Peter stepped forward. "Yes, ma'am, for two nights, if that's all right."

"Of course, dear. Would you like separate rooms or one together?"

"Together," I answered.

Carol nodded. "That'll be fifteen dollars, please."

Luna paid, and Carol led us upstairs. She handed us a key to a room at the far right. Inside, a small kitchen sat on the left, and a bathroom on the right. The main room housed a bunk bed, a single bed, a small TV, and a couch. It wasn't much, but it was cosy.

Luna took the top bunk. I took the bottom. Peter claimed the single bed. As I drifted to sleep, a vision filled my mind.

A man, engulfed in chains, stood before me. His face remained blurry, but his voice cut through the fog.

"Listen to me. You are in great danger. Do not trust the gods or anyone associated with them. They will bring you nothing but pain. Please, Gwen... I don't want anything to happen to you. Gwen... Gwen...GWEN!"

I woke with a start, gasping. Luna shook me awake, concern in her eyes. Peter stood in the corner, tense. Tears streaked my face, though I didn't remember crying. The room had changed everything was bathed in a sunset orange glow, bright leaves scattered around like a harvest festival.

"What happened?" I asked, my voice unsteady.

Peter hesitated. "It looked like you had a nightmare... and your powers reacted to it."

I blinked. "What?"

"Everything turned harvest-themed," he said, gesturing around.

I shook my head. "I heard a voice... a man in chains. He warned me not to trust the gods. He said they would only bring pain."

Luna and Peter exchanged glances.

Luna spoke first. "It's not unusual, Gwen. Every new half-blood loses control of their abilities now and then. As for the man you saw... I don't know who he is. But if he's telling you to turn against the gods, he can't be good. Be careful who you trust. It could lead to something dangerous. But I promise you're safe with us. Me and Peter will protect you. We're your friends."

Peter nodded in agreement.

I exhaled. "Thanks, guys."

Still shaken, I followed them downstairs for breakfast. Carol had prepared a feast pancakes, strawberries, bacon, toast, eggs, everything we could want.

"Really, there's no need to thank me," Carol said. "I just wish my late husband Dennis and I had children."

"I'm sorry," I murmured.

Then, I hesitated before asking, "Carol, do you know anyone who could help us? We need to get far out of state as fast as possible."

She tapped her chin. "You might try the man who lives across from me. He calls himself a traveller. If anyone knows shortcuts across states, it's him."

We finished eating and headed next door. Peter knocked on the oak door, but there was no answer. Just as we turned to leave, a deep voice called from inside.

"Enter."

We stepped in cautiously. A tall man with dark skin and sharp features sat in a chair, dressed simply in black sandals. He studied us before speaking.

"Take a seat, children. Tell me how I can help you."

A chill ran down my spine. Something about this felt bigger than us, more dangerous. And as we prepared to speak, "We're sorry to disturb you, Sir," Luna said. "We heard you were a bit of a traveler and know how to get out of state fast. You see, we need to get to California within two weeks."

The man paused for a while, then said, "Get to California in two weeks, you say? Ha ha, so little Half-Bloods, you've come seeking the winged herald's aid, have you?"

We stopped, shocked for a moment, until Luna spoke up.

"Wait... if you're the... Oh my gods, you're Hermes, God of Travelers and Thieves, and also the Messenger of Gods?"

"Yes, and you're my half-sister, little Luna," Hermes replied with a knowing smile.

"Lord Hermes," Peter said, "forgive us, my Lord, we didn't know, but could you please help us?"

"Of course," Hermes said. "I have a way to get you a good couple of states over quite quickly. However, you'll be on your own from there. I will also provide you with a map that should guide you toward the Underworld in the state of California. Consider it a favor from the God of Travelers."

"Thank you, my Lord," we all said in unison.

Hermes spoke again, "Meet me on the outskirts tomorrow. We leave then."

We went back to the inn and decided to get some rest, anticipating the morning.

HELP FROM THE GOD OF TRAVELER'S

We woke up the next morning feeling both excited and exhausted. Thankfully, I hadn't had another dream that sent my powers spiralling out of control. I still didn't fully understand how they worked or how to control them, and I had Cronus to thank for that.

After getting dressed, we headed downstairs for one last breakfast. Luna ordered an English breakfast, Peter stuck with toast, and I chose pancakes. I needed something comforting before facing whatever Hermes had planned. The God of Travelers could send us anywhere, and the uncertainty gnawed at me.

Once we finished eating, we stopped by to speak with Miss Jones before leaving. It still felt strange to call her by her first name. My mother had always insisted on addressing elders with respect, using titles like "Sir" or "Madam."

In the front room, we handed back Miss Jones's keys and thanked her for hosting us. She waved us off with a warm smile.

"There's no need to thank me, little ones," she said. "Just promise me one thing."

"Anything," Luna said.

"Be safe out there. And come back to visit sometime? It gets lonely here, and I've loved having you around. You brought a spark back to this old lady's life."

A heavy silence followed. None of us knew what lay ahead, and we couldn't promise we'd return. Luna and Peter hesitated, but I finally spoke.

"Of course, we'll come back. It's been nice here... makes me wish I could have met my grandmother."

Misses Jones teared up at that. "Oh... thank you, dear. That means a lot to me."

We shared a heartfelt hug before saying our final goodbyes. As we stepped away, Luna turned to me. "That was a kind thing to say, Gwen. But do you really intend to keep that promise? There's a huge chance we'll never see her again."

I met her gaze. "Yes. I keep my word. No matter what."

She nodded, and we made our way to the edge of the hamlet, where Hermes waited.

When he saw us, a slight smirk crossed his face. "Ah, so you showed up after all. I wasn't sure you would. You have no idea what will happen once you reach the Underworld, do you? Your mother will be freed, sure... but Gwen, you'll take her place as a prisoner in Tartarus, right alongside your treacherous, kin-devouring father."

We hadn't thought that far ahead. And maybe Hermes was right. Every time someone compared me to Cronus, the words cut deep. The thought that I might be like him, that I could hurt the people I cared about it haunted me.

But before I could respond, Luna did something I never expected. She turned on Hermes, a literal Olympian, and shouted at him.

"How dare you say that? You might be a god, but look at yourself! You're tormenting a twelve-year-old girl! Is that what the mighty Olympians have been reduced to? Bullying a child because they're scared of her? I won't let her be thrown into Tartarus for something I know she'd never do! Yes, her father is evil, and yes, her powers are a challenge, but she doesn't deserve this. Whatever happened to innocent until proven guilty?"

Her outburst stunned me. She stood up for me... but she also called my powers a problem. Did that mean she saw them as something dark? Dangerous? Just like Cronus?

Hermes studied her calmly. "I'm just stating facts, little girl. I don't care who your father is. I am an Olympian. Watch your words. You're lucky I'm more level-headed than the others. I hope you have a plan because Zeus will demand Gwen be thrown into Tartarus to prevent the prophecy."

Peter stepped forward. "What even is this prophecy? Can't you at least tell us?"

Hermes shook his head. "Sorry, kid. I took a vow, like the other Olympians. I can't speak of it."

The silence stretched between us until he added, "But believe it or not, Gwen, not all the gods are against you. Three Olympians support you."

I froze. Luna and Peter looked just as stunned as if they'd never imagined such a thing. Their disbelief stung a little, but considering how most gods had treated me so far, I couldn't blame them.

Luna, regaining her composure, addressed Hermes more formally. "Lord Hermes, please forgive my rudeness. Could you tell us which Olympians are on Gwen's side?"

Hermes considered for a moment before answering. "You're forgiven, little sister. The three who support Gwen are Artemis, goddess of the hunt; Athena, goddess of wisdom and battle strategy; and Poseidon, god of the sea, earthquakes, and horses."

Hearing that felt like a lifeline. I wasn't entirely alone. Sometimes, it even felt like Luna and Peter doubted me because of my powers. But this? This meant something.

Luna nodded. "Thank you, my lord. It's good to know we have some allies. That's better than nothing."

"No problem," Hermes said. "Now, let's get you set up."

He pulled out a rolled parchment and handed it to Luna. "This map will guide you, especially once you reach California. It'll glow when you're close to the Palace of Death and the entrance to the Underworld. Guard it with your lives."

Then he turned to me. "Look, don't take my words from earlier too harshly. I tend to speak before thinking a bad habit. Truth is, I do feel for you, Gwen. You didn't ask for any of this, but it's what you're stuck with. That's a heavy burden."

He reached into his pocket and pulled out a small green orb. Handing it to me, he said, "Give this to your mother. Tell her to smash it on the ground while thinking of home. It'll send her to the place she feels safest."

Tears burned in my eyes. "So... this will help me save her?"

"Yes," he confirmed. "But it will only rescue her. Figuring out how to get yourself out? That's on you. Be careful. The Underworld is unforgiving."

We thanked him, and he stepped back. "Alright, time to open your portal. You'll land a few states over, but I can't say which ones. Once you reach California, use the map it'll lead you straight to the Palace of Death."

White wings sprouted from his sandals, and in a blur, he sped around us, kicking up a golden tornado. When the dust settled, we stood at the edge of a vast field with a narrow road stretching ahead. On the other side of the road there was a huge forest of clustered trees.

I glanced at Luna and Peter. "What do we do now?"

Luna tightened her grip on the map. "We walk. That's all we can do."

With that, we stepped onto the road, heading toward our fate which remained uncertain to us.

HUNTED BY POWERFUL BEAST

We walked along the deserted road with the open fields on one side and the huge forest on the other. I decided I needed to learn how to summon my weapon more effectively. So far, it had appeared only by blind luck whenever I needed it most. I removed the necklace from my neck and studied it more closely. It was a silver chain with small amethyst gemstones, and at its center, a large orange sapphire gleamed. I was shocked. I'd had this necklace for ages but only noticed it now. I removed the necklace from my neck and began reaching for the sapphire, I tried to summon my sickle, but to my disappointment, nothing happened. There was no glow and No magic so reluctantly I placed it back around my neck.

Luna shot me a confused look. "Gwen, what are you doing?"

I sighed, feeling defeated. "I'm trying to summon my weapon more deliberately. I can't keep relying on luck. It might put me or the group in danger."

Luna and Peter exchanged glances, then burst into laughter. I didn't get it. After a moment, Luna spoke up.

"Cowgirl, you only just discovered you're a Half-Blood. Peter and I have known our whole lives, so we've had time to hone our abilities. You can't expect to master it in a couple of days."

I supposed she was right, but it had been a while since she'd used my nickname. "Cowgirl? It's been a while since you called me that. Thunderhead."

She raised an eyebrow. "Thunderhead? Let me guess it's because I'm the daughter of Zeus, and I can summon lightning, right?"

I smiled at her. "Yep. You got it. But I'll say this: I need to give my weapon a name."

Peter glanced at me, surprised. "You want to name your weapon? Really?"

Luna elbowed him playfully. I nodded. "I hate calling it just 'weapon.' I think I'll call it (Χρόνοι θεριστής)"

Luna grinned. "Times Reaper? I get it because Cronus is the God of Time. I like it."

We all laughed, feeling like everything was normal again like the good times at the Fort, laughing around the bonfire.

But then Peter's voice cut through the moment. "Hush! We've been walking for a while. Don't you hear those sounds?"

Luna and I exchanged confused glances. "I don't hear anything," Luna said.

Peter's face grew more worried. "We're not alone. Something is hunting us, but I don't know what."

My heart began to race. Luna and I scanned our surroundings but couldn't see or hear anything. I turned to Peter. "Are you sure? Can you sense where it is? What it is?"

He spoke in a hushed tone, his voice filled with dread. "Yes, it's hunting us. But it's not human, or any natural animal for that matter. It's a mythical monster. I just don't know where it is."

We stood in silence for a moment, and then Luna spoke. "We need to keep moving. But stay alert. Let's head into the trees."

We moved into the dense forest, hoping we'd be safe. But the thick canopy blocked the sunlight, plunging the woods into an eerie darkness. The atmosphere felt suffocating, like we'd wandered into a haunted place. Every snap of a twig, every hiss of a snake sent a chill down my spine. Then, a growl a deep, rumbling sound like that of a lion echoed through the trees. I also heard the unmistakable sound of a mountain goat. What could be following us?

Fear set in. My heart pounded. My mind raced. And then I saw the look of horror on Peter's face.

"Guys," Peter said, his voice trembling. "We need to get out of here. Back into the light. It was a mistake to come in here."

Luna frowned. "What do you mean? I thought we'd be safer here."

"No," Peter said, his voice shaking. "We made it worse. Listen. First, we heard a hiss. Then a growl. Then something like a mountain goat. Put it together what creature fits that description?"

Luna and I paused. It hit us like a ton of bricks. "The Chimera," I whispered, my voice quivering.

Just as I spoke, a deafening roar shook the forest. Luna grabbed us and shot us back into the open road with lightning.

I froze. The Chimera stood before us its massive lion body, a goat's head, and a snake's tail. The very sight paralyzed me. Luna shouted, "Stay on guard! Prepare for battle!"

Peter and Luna summoned their weapons instantly, but when I tried, nothing happened.

"Great," I thought. "Just when I need you the most."

"I can't summon my weapon. It's not working," I shouted to Luna.

"It's fine. Stay behind us. Peter and I can handle this."

Luna hurled her thunderbolts at the Chimera, but it dodged, and the bolts set the trees ablaze, creating a massive fire.

Peter barked orders. "Watch out for its tail! The snake's mouth is venomous, and the goat head can breathe fire!"

Luna and Peter fought bravely, but the Chimera relished the hunt. It leapt and slashed Luna with its powerful claws. She crashed to the ground, right on top of Peter. They were vulnerable, and I screamed in fury.

As I screamed, time seemed to freeze. The Chimera, the fire, the forest all halted in place. Only Peter and Luna were unaffected.

"GWEN, NO!" Luna shouted.

But it was too late. My weapon appeared in my hand Times Reaper, glowing orange. With one swift motion, I sliced through the Chimera, disintegrating it with a blast of light.

When time resumed, Luna's voice broke through my thoughts. "Gwen, remember what we said. Be careful when using your abilities. The Gods of

Olympus are already watching you. They'll fear you more if you keep using them."

Anger boiled inside me. "Are you serious? Did you forget that I just saved you? Again?" I snapped. "You guys use your powers all the time. Why can't I use mine? Just because some gods are up there getting scared?"

Peter tried to reason with me. "You don't know how to control your powers yet. We don't want to give Olympus another reason to hate you. We'll help you master them, but we need to do it under Chiron's supervision, at the Fort."

I understood what they meant, but the frustration was overwhelming. I had just saved their lives from a monster. "Whatever," I muttered.

And deep down, I couldn't shake the feeling that the prophecy was coming true that the Gods were already suspicious of me.

We gave Luna some ambrosia to heal her wounds, then continued on the road. As we walked, a man on a blood-red motorcycle appeared. The bike was decorated with swords and weapons, almost like something from a medieval battlefield.

"Need a lift, kids?" he called in a menacing tone. "I can take you to the nearest gas station."

Visit From War Itself

We all exchanged glances, discussing what to do next. The guy in front of us looked like he belonged to a biker gang. He had a black military-style haircut, pale skin, and a face covered in scars, as though he had just returned from a brutal war. His black sunglasses hid his eyes, and he wore black jeans, a black shirt, and a black leather jacket adorned with spikes. Luna spoke up first. "I don't think we should trust this guy. Look at him; he just gives off bad vibes. This is raising alarm bells in my head. Let's walk away." She made a valid point. He definitely had a dangerous aura.

Peter chimed in next. "I think we should take him up on his offer."

"WHAT?" Luna exclaimed, her voice rising.

Peter hushed her. "Think about it. I know he looks shady, but consider this: if we keep walking, who knows how long it'll take to get to the nearest gas station? Not to mention, who knows how many monsters will attack us along the way? We're on a deadline, and we're already losing track of time."

Peter made some solid points. We were on a time crunch, and if we kept walking, monsters could keep attacking us. As much as we didn't want to trust the guy, we didn't have many other options.

The man spoke again. "I haven't got all day, kids. Are you coming or not? I'm a busy man, and I've got places to be. So, you in or out?"

"Just a minute," I said, then turned to Peter, who was already making up his mind.

"I know it's a risk, but this is our best shot," Peter said. "Look, I don't like this either, but you've got to take my word for it. Sometimes you have to trust people, even if they look like trouble."

Reluctantly, Luna agreed, and I turned to the man. "Okay, we'll take you up on your offer. Thanks."

He simply said, "Hey, no problem, kid. Glad I could be of service."

Despite his words, I couldn't shake the bad feeling in my gut. It felt like his very soul was drenched in conflict, pain, and a thirst for battle.

We climbed onto his motorcycle and sped down the road. The man broke the silence, asking, "So, what brings you kids out here? It's not common for kids to be wandering out here in the middle of nowhere."

"Believe us, sir, you wouldn't believe us if we told you," I replied.

He laughed, but it was unsettling. It sounded like the laugh of a psychopath. After a moment, he said, "Kid, I've seen my fair share of strange stuff. Try me. I've seen weirder things than you can imagine."

I didn't know how to respond. How could we tell him the truth? The real truth? Thankfully, Luna spoke up, saying, "Sorry, sir, but we can't tell you why we're out here. We have a good reason, but you wouldn't believe us, so it's better if we keep it to ourselves."

The man didn't respond right away. After a long pause, he said, "Fair enough, little ones. Forgive me. I didn't mean to get personal. I'm not much of a conversationalist unless we're on a bloodstained battlefield."

"So, you're a soldier?" I asked.

He smiled, a cold grin. "Actually, I'm more like a commander. The one who leads strong men into battle."

"Just men?" Luna asked.

"Yep. I only train and lead men. No offense, but I don't believe women belong on the battlefield. Now, my sister, on the other hand, she'll take anyone, though you've got to prove yourself to her first."

Luna scowled. "No offense, sir, but that's a little sexist. Girls are just as capable on a battlefield as men."

He gave Luna a sharp look in the side mirror. "Maybe so, but I don't care what you think, little one. Right or wrong, I won't train a woman to fight on the battlefield. War is a masculine thing, not a feminine one. Understand?"

I saw Luna's face redden with anger. She muttered under her breath, "This sexist piece of work is making me so angry."

I grabbed her arm and whispered in her ear, "I know, believe me. I get it. But just hold on. Once we get to the next gas station, we'll part ways. We won't have to talk to him anymore."

She sighed. "Yeah, okay. I'm lucky I've got you here to calm me down. Otherwise, I might just kill this sexist man."

We laughed at that, but the man suddenly spoke. "Alright, you clowns, what's so funny back there?"

"Oh, nothing much, sir. Just girl talk," I said, trying to lighten the mood.

A while later, we spotted a gas station in the distance, with a small diner in front of it called "Burger Diner." The man turned to us and asked, "How about I treat you to some burgers?"

We all thought for a moment. We were hungry, so Peter replied, "Yes, thank you, sir."

When we arrived, the diner was practically empty, except for one chef in the kitchen and a nice old lady at the cashier. The man went to order the burgers, and we sat at a red-seated booth that looked like something out of a 1950s diner. For me, it was oddly funny; it reminded me of when my mom and I would watch films together during storms, or if one of us was upset, or when we were just bored on a long day. The man finished ordering and came back, sitting opposite us. He smiled and said, "Well, kids, now there's nothing to do but wait."

We all thanked him, and then the silence took over. Luna couldn't stand it for long and broke it by questioning the man. "Look, sir, it's not that we're not grateful for your help, but why are you helping us? I mean, you don't even know us. You literally just picked up three random kids on your bike and bought us food. It's a little creepy."

The man paused, then gave Luna an eerie, sinister grin that slowly turned into a disturbing smile. "Fair enough," he said. "I thought you kids could use a break after that Chimera attack. Good thing you had that Ambrosia on you. Works miracles, doesn't it?"

We were all stunned. How could he know about the Chimera? It should have been hidden by Hecate's magic.

He was still looking at us with the same sinister grin as he spoke. "What's the matter, kids? Snake got your tongue, or are you all trying to wrap your tiny, insignificant little minds around how I know about that?"

Peter was about to ask how he knew when the nice old lady brought over our food. The man then said, "Tell you what, I'll tell you how I know after we finish eating this delicious food in front of us."

We all didn't like it, but we were hungry, and it would've been a shame to waste the food. So, we agreed, reluctantly. And honestly, the food was amazing. The burger was juicy, perfectly seasoned, with a nice grill on it. The fries were crispy and seasoned with sea salt and vinegar. It made my mouth water. To top it off, a large Coca-Cola Zero. Honestly, it was all so delicious.

After we finished, Luna's impatience grew, and she demanded, "Okay, you've eaten your food. Now spill. How can you see through Hecate's magic and know about the Chimera attack? Are you stalking us or something?"

The man snarled. "To answer your questions in order: Number one, because I'm not a stupid mortal, and two, I see and know all the battles and wars that happen on this earth. It's kind of my thing."

Peter spoke up, "How is that possible if you're not mortal? Then what, or who, are you?"

The man started laughing, then took off his black sunglasses. What I saw made my skin crawl. His eyes were made of molten lava, glowing with fire. Just looking at him filled me with terror, like I was staring into the embodiment of war and death. I wanted to speak, but we were all frozen in fear.

Eventually, I managed to speak in a quivering voice. "W...who are you?"

The man laughed harder, like he'd lost his mind. Eventually, he stopped, looking at us and saying, "Who am I, little one? You really don't know, do you? I'm Ares, son of Zeus, one of the twelve Olympians. I am the embodiment of the dark side of war; God of War, bloodshed, and courage. That's who I am."

I was speechless. This whole time, we'd been talking to Ares.

Finally, I found my voice and asked, "So you're Ares. Can I ask you something?"

Peter and Luna looked at me like I'd just made the worst decision, but it was too late. Ares stared at me and said, "Sure, little one. What do you want to know?"

I hesitated, knowing one wrong word might get me killed, but I forced myself to ask, "What is it you want from us?"

I froze as soon as I asked the question, and so did Peter and Luna. Ares thought for a moment, then replied coldly, "What I want, Daughter of Cronus, is very simple; either your immediate death or your immediate surrender to Lord Hades so you may join your father in Tartarus and suffer unimaginable torture."

Immediately, Peter and Luna summoned their weapons and held them to Ares's throat. Luna, her eyes blazing with fury, said, "Don't you dare talk to her like that. We won't let you lay even a finger on her. Not unless you want to anger Lord Zeus and Lady Athena by killing their children."

Ares paused, sighed, and said, "Do you know how many children Zeus has, little one? Too many, and he doesn't care about them. Didn't you anger him recently by helping that Titan spawn? Half-Blood? Don't make me laugh."

Luna lowered her head, frustration and defeat showing.

Ares smiled. "That's what I thought. The only one I realistically have to worry about is my stuck-up sister Athena. I can't understand why she, along with Artemis and Poseidon, is supporting you. You're just a child of the kin-eating monster."

While Luna and Peter continued to argue with Ares, I drifted into my own thoughts, overwhelmed by guilt and anger. Thoughts of how I was the reason my mother was suffering in Hades's realm kept swirling in my mind.

Finally, I couldn't take it anymore. I screamed, "SHUT UP! WILL YOU ALL JUST SHUT UP FOR THE LOVE OF ZEUS!"

Everyone froze. Ares glared at me with fury in his eyes, while Peter and Luna stared at me in shock.

Ares was the first to speak. "You dare speak to a God of Olympus that way, Titan spawn?"

I didn't care. "I don't care. I really don't. My mom's rotting in Hades because of me, and I can't escape the thoughts in my head. That I'm just like Cronus, I can't make those thoughts stop. The second half of the prophecy is coming true, and we still haven't figured out how to get out of the Underworld. So just shut the hell up."

Peter and Luna watched me, sympathy and concern in their eyes. Luna hugged me tightly, whispering, "Gwen, I... I'm so sorry."

I just remember sobbing after that into Luna's shoulder. Peter turned to Ares and said, "Listen, my Lord, I think it's best for all of us if you leave. Gwen's not like Cronus. We will get her mother out of the Underworld, and we won't surrender her either." Ares just stared at us for a couple of seconds, then eventually said, "Fine. I can't be bothered anyway. If I don't get you, either the Harpies or Hades will, and I hope for your sake, the Harpies get their hands on you before Hades does."

I don't remember much after that. I know something else was said, but I ended up passing out in Luna's arms. When I woke up, I was in the back of a moving van with Luna and Peter. Luna first noticed me and said, "You're awake finally. How are you feeling?" I felt dizzy but managed to say, "I'm okay, thanks. But where are we?" Peter responded, "We're in the back of a van Ares put us in, heading to Kansas. From there, we should be able to find transport further west to California."

Okay, all of this was making sense so far. At least for now, we had a small plan. I asked, "Where are we now?" Luna said, "Iowa. We haven't long left to dinner, so we still got a while to go, about six hours at least." We all sat in thought for a moment, then Peter spoke up and said, "This might be a blessing in disguise. We can make a proper plan on how to get out of the Underworld with everybody."

We thought about it and agreed, which made me happy. We were officially making a definite plan on how to deal with Hades and the Underworld.

THE ROAD TRIP PLAN

We all sat next to each other in the van. For a moment, we sat in silence, but I began to notice something; Peter and Luna kept glancing at me with worried eyes. It bothered me, and I wasn't sure whether to ask them what was wrong. I decided to push it to the back of my mind.

Eventually, Peter spoke up. "Right, should we make a start on our plan? We're going to need it if we're going to escape the Underworld."

Luna agreed. "I agree. After all, not a lot of people have survived the Underworld. In fact, only a handful made it out, most with help from some gods and goddesses, and a lot of luck from Tyche, the Goddess of Luck."

"So," I said, "we just need to do the same thing they did. Easy, right?"

Luna looked uneasy. "It's not as simple as that, Gwen. Like I said, most escaped with help and a lot of luck. Hades' realm is full of traps and monsters. This won't be simple. In and out doesn't work like that; not in the Underworld."

Peter suggested, "Right, if that's the case, let's go over what we know about the Underworld. That way, we can make strong suggestions on the best course of action when we get there. And most importantly, how we deal with its king."

We all nodded and agreed, so we began going over what we knew about the Underworld. Peter started by telling us about its origins. "The first thing to exist was Tartarus. It was a child of Chaos, the first ever thing to exist. It was a tough, fiery embodiment of destruction, pain, and torment, deep under Gaea."

We listened intently as Luna continued from Peter, "After the war between the Olympians and the Titans, the three brothers, Zeus, Poseidon, and Hades, drew lots to see who got which realm."

I picked up the story. "Yeah, Zeus drew the biggest lot, so he became the King of Olympus and, by extension, King of the Olympian gods and goddesses. Poseidon got the middle lot, so he took control of the ocean from the Titan Oceanus and became the King of the Ocean and Atlantis. And Hades got the shortest string, which made him the ruler of the Underworld, the King of the Dead. With the help of the five rivers beneath Gaia, he created the other two dimensions of the Underworld: The Fields of Asphodel, where souls go if they lived ordinary lives, and Elysium, the perfect paradise for heroes who served the Olympians."

Luna looked at me, surprised. "Wow, Gwen, I forgot you loved Greek mythology before you knew it was real."

Peter then spoke up, "Right. Let's press on. The entrance to the Underworld, like Chiron said, is located in a building called the Palace of Death. It's a little on the nose, but from there, we should find Charon, the ferryman. If we give him some drachmas, he should take us through the River Styx and into the Fields of Asphodel, where Hades' castle is located. However, there's no guarantee he'll get us back out of the Underworld."

Luna replied, "Agreed. And Gwen only got one orb from Hermes, and that's for her mom. Not to mention, Hades' castle is on the far edge of Asphodel. Running back to the entrance is impossible." This was a real problem. Even if we got to the Underworld, with all the monsters, it would be difficult to reach Hades' castle. And we had no way to escape if we did.

I had a suggestion, but I knew it wouldn't be well received. I turned to Peter and Luna and asked, "I have a suggestion, but you probably won't like it."

Luna turned to me and said, "Go ahead. We'll hear you out. At least you're a Half-Blood, too. No matter what Olympus says."

I took a deep breath, gathering my courage. "If I practice a little more, I should be able to master my ability to slow down time for a long period. It might give us the chance to escape. We can pretend to give me up, and when my mom is safe, I'll slow down time. That'll give us time to run back to Charon. I'm sure if we pay him extra, he'll wait for us."

They didn't say anything for a long time, but their expressions said it all. They weren't on board with this decision. The very mention of using my powers frightened them. I couldn't fully blame them, but it still hurt. Luna, especially, had been my friend since we were little kids, and every time I mentioned using my powers, she gave me a look; like I was going to use them for evil, just like Cronus. But it was the best idea we had, and they just couldn't see it.

Eventually, Luna spoke up. "No, Gwen. Absolutely not. Like we said, we don't need the gods to have another reason to hate you."

I replied angrily, "To Tartarus with the gods. You have to admit, this is the best plan we've got. Why are you both so against me? I thought we were friends. No, wait, I know; it's because I'm the daughter of Cronus, right?"

They both remained silent for a while. I screamed at them, "ANSWER ME! AM I RIGHT? I SWEAR THE

SECOND PART OF THE PROPHECY IS COMING TRUE BY THE SECOND! JUST TELL ME I'M RIGHT!"

Luna shouted back, "NO!" When I looked at her, she was crying. She then said, still crying, "No, Gwen. It's not because you're the daughter of Cronus. I know I've been acting differently, but it's not because of that. It's because I don't want them to kill you. If you grow strong enough, Zeus will kill you, and if he does, I don't know what I'll do."

Luna calmed herself down and looked at me. I didn't know how to respond. But what I did say was this: "I understand that the gods want me dead, and I understand that growing too powerful will make Zeus hate me more. But we don't exactly have a better idea, and I can't stay weak forever. Please."

Luna replied, "Sorry, Gwen, but we can't do that. We'll find another way, I promise. But for now, please..."

I remember thinking this was like talking to a brick wall. I realised they were never going to allow me to use my powers. "Okay, fine," I said in an annoyed tone. I stayed angry for a while after that. We all sat in silence in our own respective corners. I could tell they wanted to talk about it more, and truth be told, I wanted to talk about it more too. I didn't want to be angry with them, but they weren't leaving me many options. I promised myself that by the time we were in the Underworld, if we didn't have a way out, I would use my powers, despite the gods' hatred and despite what Luna and Peter thought.

I shut my eyes and fell asleep for a while. I remember hearing that same voice from my dream back when we stayed with Carol Jones. It was the same voice of the man who was chained up, though this time, I couldn't see him. He said to me, "Gwen, listen to me. Don't listen to them. If you want to survive the Underworld, you need to trust in yourself and your own power. It's your power, not theirs, not your father's. It's your power."

Once he said that, I woke up. Thankfully, nothing had changed in the van, but Luna was looking at me. She asked, "Gwen, you're awake. Were you having another dream about that man? I noticed your eyes were glowing orange while you were asleep."

I thought for a moment. Whether or not I should tell her the truth, it would just concern her more if I mentioned I was talking to the same man again. So, I decided to lie. "No, I wasn't. I'm not sure why my eyes were glowing, though."

Luna looked at me like she knew I wasn't telling her the truth, but she wasn't willing to argue with me again. She wasn't going to press me on it. "How long was I asleep?" I asked.

Peter replied, "A good couple of hours. Luna and I are still thinking about the best way to get out of the Underworld."

I gathered they weren't going to go with my plan, but I sucked it up and just went with it. I would do whatever it took, no matter the cost.

Luna eventually looked up and said, "Gwen, can I ask you something?"

I looked at her and said, "Of course, Thunder Brain. Ask me anything." I don't think this was the time for nicknames, though. She didn't look too impressed with my comment.

She hesitated before continuing, "What did you mean by the second half of the prophecy coming true by the second? I thought you told us the full prophecy already."

Her question caught me off guard. I didn't know whether I should tell her the real prophecy. Luna continued, "It's not the first time you mentioned it either. You also brought it up at the diner when you were yelling at Ares. So, I take it you haven't told us the full prophecy, have you?"

I looked down, feeling kind of bad. But I didn't want to believe the final part of the prophecy. Still, I felt like, in that moment, I had no choice but to tell the truth. "No, I didn't tell you the full prophecy. I only told you the first half."

Peter and Luna both looked concerned. After a long pause, Peter asked, "Can you please tell us the full prophecy, Gwen? If this quest is going to work, we need to know the full prophecy."

I hesitated for a long while. I didn't know how they'd react, and I didn't want to admit the truth because it felt like I'd be confirming the prophecy's power. But in the end, I couldn't avoid it anymore. I finally told them the full prophecy:

"You shall go West and find the doors to the Dark one's realm.
You shall find your mother and see her safely returned to the overworld.
You shall be looked at with fear and suspicion by those you love and cherish the most.
And find yourself lost and alone when your story is complete."

As I recited the prophecy, I heard those words in my head again, repeating over and over. Luna and Peter thought for a while after I finished telling them the prophecy. Finally, Luna said, "That's why, Gwen. Why didn't you tell us? This isn't exactly a minor detail after all."

Her accusation made me lose control. I snapped at her. "Well, considering how this has gone so far, what did you expect? All you've done is look at my powers with suspicion. I bet you're frightened right now, after all, you were watching my eyes glow while I was asleep. You can say what you want, but I don't doubt you want to protect me. You can't deny that's what you've been doing."

Luna didn't even look at me. She just said, "Yeah, sorry," and didn't say another word.

Peter then said, "We'll have to worry about this another time. We're coming up close to Kansas. I think we can plan to go further East, maybe catch a bus that'll take us further out. Let's grab some food while we're at it."

Luna and I agreed that some food would calm us down. I felt bad, but I had to be honest with myself; it's just how I felt. I turned to Luna and said, "Look, I'm sorry. It's just hard to see this any other way, especially with the prophecy."

Luna looked at me and said, "Yeah, I'm sorry too. I don't like us fighting. We've been like sisters since we were very young, and I don't want to lose that. Shall we let bygones be bygones?"

I nodded, and she hugged me. The van's doors opened, and we stepped out. Peter said, "Well, we're here. This is Kansas. Let's see what this place has in store for us."

I thought to myself, *Bring it on. Let's see how far we can go before something crazy happens again.* We laughed and walked on, ready to take on whatever comes next.

THEY COME FOR ME AGAIN

We looked around the city, taking in its beauty. The bright yellow sun beat down, casting warm rays over the tall buildings. The sky stood clear and blue, with not a cloud in sight. The buildings offered just enough shade to relieve the sun's heat, and the breeze from the nearby beach cooled the air. This would've been the perfect place to relax if it weren't for our danger.

I turned to Luna with a grin. "Hey, maybe when this nightmare is over, we could come back here for a holiday. Do a bit of sunbathing. What do you think?"

Luna shot me a playful grin. "Sure, cowgirl. Why not? We could even go on a shopping spree. It'd be a nice little girls' trip."

We laughed, the sound ringing through the street. It felt like the carefree days before everything fell apart. Peter joined in, shaking his head.

"What about me?" he said. "Don't tell me you're planning a holiday without me after everything we've been through."

We laughed harder, teasing him more. Luna looked at Peter, her smile mischievous. "Of course, you can come, Peter. But you'll have to be our honorary girl for the trip."

Peter's face turned bright pink, and we poked fun at him again. Once the teasing died, we shifted our attention to our situation.

"We should probably figure out exactly where we are," I suggested. We had to be cautious not to reveal we were alone, especially since we were just kids. An older woman was sitting on a bench nearby, feeding some birds. She looked harmless enough, so we decided to ask her.

I approached her first. "Excuse me, miss?" She looked up from her feeding, her voice soft but warm.

"Yes, my dears. How can I help you?" she asked.

Luna stepped forward, her tone polite but cautious. "We're sorry to bother you, but can you tell us where we are?"

The woman smiled kindly. "Of course, dears. You're in Topeka, the capital of Kansas."

I exhaled in relief. We finally knew where we were. Peter quickly asked, "Do you know if there's a bus heading to California? We're meeting some family there."

She paused, thinking for a moment before responding, her voice gentle. "Yes, there's a bus that travels from here to California. It passes through Colorado, Utah, and Nevada before reaching Los

Angeles. The next bus leaves tomorrow morning at 8:00 AM."

We thanked her, and after a brief moment of silent exchange, we decided to find somewhere safe to stay for the night. Peter was the first to bring up the reality of our situation.

"That's all well and good," he said, looking uneasy, "but what do we do for tonight? We can't just stay out in the open. We may be in a city, but monsters are still a threat."

Luna scanned the area, then her eyes lit up. "We can stay at that bed and breakfast," she said, nodding toward a cozy, one-story building. "It looks safe enough."

We agreed and walked toward the bed and breakfast. The place seemed family-run, with a warm, welcoming atmosphere. We rang the bell at the front desk, and a young woman, probably around sixteen, greeted us with a bright smile.

"Hello there, little ones! How can I help you?" she asked cheerfully.

Peter spoke up. "Sorry to bother you, miss, but we just need one room for tonight. We'll be out by 7:00 AM tomorrow if that's okay."

"Of course, not a problem at all," she said. She quickly scribbled on a notepad and asked for our names and signatures, which we provided. After handing us the room key, she wished us well, and we made our way to our room. It was a peaceful walk, and you don't notice until you realize how calm it feels.

The room had a simple setup: a double bed, a small bed, a kitchen, and a bathroom. Peter spoke first, looking between Luna and me.

"You girls can take the big bed," he said, "and I'll take the small one. Is that alright with you?"

Luna raised an eyebrow and smirked. "I should hope so, Peter. There are two girls and one boy. What were you planning to do, sleep in the big bed while we fought over the small one?"

Peter stammered, trying to explain himself, but Luna cut him off, laughing. "I'm just joking! Thanks for being a gentleman. Who knew you had it in you?" Her tone was teasing but kind and Peter's face turned red.

We settled in, ordered some snacks, and tried to relax. The night grew darker, and though I was exhausted, sleep wouldn't come. My thoughts kept spinning in circles my powers, father, and mother. The guilt over what had happened, over what was happening to my mother in Hades' castle, gnawed at me. I couldn't stop thinking about it.

I didn't even notice that Luna had woken up and was watching me. Her voice, soft but full of concern, broke through my spiral.

"Gwen, is something bothering you?" she asked quietly. "You know you can talk to me, right?"

I let out a long breath, feeling the weight of everything. "It's just... everything that's happened, Luna. My powers feel like a curse, and my father... he's Cronus. My mother's stuck in Hades because of me. I don't know what to do. I can't keep this up."

Luna sat up; her expression thoughtful. "None of us asked to be Half-Bloods, Gwen. We didn't choose this life. It's unfair, I know. Monsters at every turn, the constant fight for survival... But we will get your mother back. We'll figure out your powers. And we'll prove to Zeus that you're not the curse everyone thinks you are. I promise."

Her words, warm and full of reassurance, helped ease the knot in my chest. I smiled, feeling a bit lighter. "Thanks, Thunderhead."

"No problem, cowgirl," she said with a wink.

I hugged her momentarily before whispering, "I'm going out for some fresh air." She nodded and fell asleep as I quietly slipped out of the room.

I paced around the building, trying to shake off the weight of my thoughts. I walked in circles, hoping the movement would tire me enough to sleep. But after a while, it became monotonous. I decided to walk further down the street. The night felt heavy with silence, and I couldn't stop thinking about my mother, wishing I could change everything. If I could, I would give up anything to return to the farm, have an everyday life, and forget all this madness.

Eventually, I sat on a bench, trying to calm my racing thoughts. I wasn't sure when, but exhaustion finally overcame me, and I drifted off into a light sleep. When I opened my eyes, the moon hung high in the sky, casting an eerie glow over everything. It took a moment for me to realise that I had been out there for hours. I needed to return, Luna and Peter would be worried by now. As I stood to leave, I noticed two figures standing near the entrance of the bed and breakfast. My heart sank when I recognised them: Amanda and Victoria. I ducked behind a corner, but it was too late.

"I see you, Gwen," Amanda called, her voice cold and taunting. "You might as well come out now, little Titan."

I stepped out, heart pounding. I walked toward them, half-afraid and half-filled with adrenaline. Victoria wasn't ready to attack, but her eyes held a menacing glint.

"Don't worry, little one," Victoria said with a smirk. "I'm not going to attack you this time. I just came with a warning. You'd do well to listen."

I narrowed my eyes, trying to keep my voice steady. "A warning? What could you possibly have to say?"

Victoria laughed wickedly. "Stay off that bus tomorrow, Gwen. Unless you want your friends to die. Zeus is tired of your little escapes. He's sending someone stronger, and you do not want to face them so I ask you one more surrender to us."

I didn't flinch. "No. I'm getting my mother back, and that's the end of it. I won't surrender to a monster like you."

Victoria's smile faltered, but only slightly. "Alright, little one. It's your funeral. Just don't say I didn't warn you. And tell your Half-Blood friends I said hello."

Before I could react, they disappeared, vanishing into the night.

I sprinted back to the room, my heart racing. Luna and Peter were waiting for me; concern etched on their faces.

"Where have you been?" Luna asked. "You've been gone for two hours! I thought you'd been captured."

I was out of breath, trying to steady myself. "You don't want to know. I had a little chat with Amanda and Victoria. They gave me a warning."

Luna and Peter exchanged glances, but they didn't press. I was exhausted, and so were they. We decided to leave it until morning.

But I couldn't shake the feeling that we were never safe. Not really.

THE GODDESSES OF VENGEANCE ATTACK

We all struggled to sleep that night. Despite how tired I was, I couldn't force myself to sleep. Luna and Peter tried, but we all stayed awake, the weight of Amanda and Victoria's warning echoing in our minds. I couldn't stop thinking about what Zeus might be sending. What could be worse than everything we had already faced? By the time we finally got up, it was 7:00 AM. I was exhausted, but I knew I had to get up. We freshened up and went to breakfast, where Luna and Peter kept staring at me. I knew what they wanted they wanted me to tell them what happened last night. But truthfully, I wasn't ready to explain it yet. The events from the night before still made no sense to me, and all the questions kept swirling in my head. Should I tell them? What could be worse than Amanda and Victoria? Why shouldn't we get on the bus?

The stress must have been visible on my face because Peter asked, "Gwen, are you okay? You don't look so good."

I wasn't okay. I was far from it. The warning haunted me had I angered the Gods of Olympus? Finally, I gathered myself and decided to tell them.

"I fell asleep on a bench. When I awoke and started heading back to the building, Amanda and Victoria were there. They told me, 'I'm giving you a warning—don't get on that bus tomorrow. Not unless you want your friends to die. Zeus has gotten tired of you getting away all the time, so he's sending someone stronger. You do not want to face these creatures, little one. I promise you. So, I'll ask you one more time to surrender to us.' I, of course, refused to surrender to them and told them I was getting my mother back. Then she said, 'Fine, just don't say I didn't warn you.' They both left, and I rushed back here. That's it." We sat in silence for what felt like hours. Luna finally broke it.

"Right. That settles it," she said her voice firm. "We are not getting on that bus."

I didn't expect those words from her. Peter immediately argued, "You're joking, right? Our deadline was TWO WEEKS! We've already lost a week. The bus is the quickest way to LA, and we have to take the risk even if it's a huge trap."

Luna looked at him, shocked and desperate. "Peter," she snapped. "Are you INSANE? Do you have a death wish?"

Peter defended himself, raising his voice. "No more than you, Luna! But what other option do we have? We have to get on that bus in 30 minutes. If we don't, Zeus will send Hades to kill Gwen's mother, and then he'll hunt Gwen himself!"

Their argument made my stomach churn. The idea that Luna and Peter could get hurt or worse, killed because of me made me feel physically sick. I felt like I might cry, scream, and throw up all at once. I couldn't focus on their words, but I knew Peter was right deep down. This was our best option.

I took a deep breath and finally spoke, trying to steady myself. "Will you both stop with this childish behavior? I'm terrified too, okay? I hate this situation, but Peter's right. We don't have much time, and this is our best option. So we need to get on that bus and be ready for a sudden attack. That's all we can do, right?"

They looked at me Peter with confidence and gratitude but Luna with concern. Her voice trembled as she spoke. "Gwen, are you sure about this? If we get on that bus, there's no turning back. If things go wrong, we'll have to fight and who knows what Zeus is sending after us?"

I met her eyes with determination. "I'm sure. I know this is risky, but we have to get to the Underworld as soon as possible. My mother's depending on me. Please trust me, Luna. This is our only choice."

Luna hesitated, but with a heavy sigh, she relented. "Okay, Gwen. If you and Peter think this is the best move, then I'll trust the group decision. We'll take the bus but we stay on high alert."

We thanked the receptionist, returned the key, and rushed to the bus stop. The bus arrived five minutes later. We scanned the area nervously, still on edge, waiting for any sign of Amanda, Victoria, or whatever else might be coming after us. The bus driver snapped us out of our trance. "You kids getting on or not?"

We nodded, climbed on, and Luna asked for three tickets to Los Angeles. She paid, and we headed toward the back of the bus. "This will be good," Luna said. "We can keep an eye out for anything strange."

I asked, "How long is the bus ride from Kansas to Los Angeles?"

Luna checked her phone. "It's 33 hours and 20 minutes one day and nine hours of travel."

Great. It was a long ride with uncomfortable seats, but at least it was the fastest way to get to LA. As the bus took off, we stayed alert, knowing an attack could come at any time. The hours dragged on. We talked about random things what we'd do when this was all over, our favorite colors, TV shows anything to distract ourselves. After twelve hours, it was dark outside. Peter turned to us.

"Are we sure there's even an ambush? Maybe Amanda and Victoria just wanted us to get worked up and wind ourselves up, so it'd be easier to attack Gwen."

We all thought about it. Peter had a point. If they were going to ambush us, why hadn't they done it yet? Could Amanda and Victoria have been lying to get us all anxious?

Luna responded, "You know, Peter, you might be right. This could just be a plot to mess with us, but it's better to be safe than sorry. Stay on guard."

As we entered Colorado, only two states away from California, we started to relax. Maybe it was all just a joke. Then, suddenly, the bus shook violently. Everyone jolted awake.

"What in all of Olympus was that?" Peter shouted.

The bus driver pulled over to investigate, but the bus exploded in a massive fireball when we stepped outside. The force of the blast threw us to the ground. Dazed and confused, we got up and checked ourselves for injuries. Thankfully, we only had a few cuts. But when we turned to Luna, she was staring in horror.

Peter asked, "What's wrong?"

Luna's voice trembled as she pointed at the top of the burning bus. "Look."

We turned and froze. Three women stood on top of the bus. Their skin was dark, covered in scars. They had black metallic wings with purple sparks at the tips. Their armor and chains shimmered in the firelight, and their hair was as dark as the night sky. Their eyes were glowing purple, and blood dripped from their wings. They wielded flaming swords that burned like wildfire. I knew who they were and didn't want to believe it. But it was unmistakable: the Punishers of Tartarus The Furies.

I whispered, "Luna, p... please tell me they're not who I think they are. Please say I'm wrong."

Luna's terrified gaze met mine. "I'm sorry, Gwen. They are exactly who you think they are. We're being attacked by the strongest beings in all of Hellenism."

Peter looked at us, panic on his face. "What do we do? We can fight, but we don't stand a chance. We're dead."

His words made my heart drop, and my whole body felt like it was going to collapse. I gripped my necklace, wishing this was all a nightmare. But then, with an orange glow, my sickle appeared in my hand.

Luna didn't hesitate. "We fight," she said. "We have to defend ourselves. We pray the gods give us some mercy tonight."

We summoned our weapons. Peter, Luna, and I prepared for the battle of our lives.

Then, one of the Furies swung her sword, sending a massive slash of red flames hurtling toward us. Luna stepped forward and shielded us with her lightning, deflecting the blast. But the force sent us flying back. As Luna recovered, she tried to strike back, but the Furies were faster, using their wings to dodge the lightning. Purple sparks filled the air as they summoned a lightning storm, hitting us all at once.

The pain was unbearable. It felt like my insides were on fire, and when the lightning stopped, we collapsed in agony. Luna tried to summon another shield, but it couldn't hold. The Furies broke through, sending us flying again. Luna passed out. Peter and I were in no better shape.

Peter's voice shook as he said, "We're dead. There's nothing left to do."

I felt myself slipping into unconsciousness, my body too weak to keep fighting. Just as everything seemed lost, I heard the sound of a horn and the Furies seemed confused, distracted by something. I couldn't focus, too weak and in pain to care about anything but relief. Then, I heard the thundering of hooves and arrows flying around the Furies. The last thing I saw before I blacked out was the Furies' confusion and the sounds of battle.

SAVED BY A FAMILIAR FRIEND

When I woke up, the sun had already risen. I looked around, realising we were at a small campsite. Luna and Peter were still asleep. The campfire in the center was nothing but charred remnants. I rushed to them, shaking them awake. "Guys, wake up, wake up!" I panicked.

It was then that I noticed something strange. My injuries, as well as Luna's and Peter's, healed entirely. It was as though we had never faced the Furies. But we knew this wasn't a dream. We hadn't fallen asleep at a campsite, and the bus was nowhere to be seen.

After a few more shakes, Peter and Luna jolted awake. They checked themselves, finding no wounds. When they were sure they were okay, Luna spoke with relief, "Gwen, you're alive... we're all alive. But how? We shouldn't have survived an attack from the Furies. You'd need to be a god to survive that."

I hugged her and Peter tightly, my voice shaky with relief. "I don't know... I woke up here, too. I don't remember what happened."

When I eventually stopped hugging them, Peter spoke up. "I'm a little concerned about who saved us, but I'm extremely relieved that we're all okay. That attack from the Furies was way too close for comfort. We all could have died in that moment. Maybe you were right, Luna. We shouldn't have gotten on that bus." We're stuck in the middle of nowhere with no clear plan. We won't make it to Los Angeles or the Underworld before the deadline. Zeus will kill Gwen's mother, and we'll be hunted by monsters."

The thought of Zeus killing my mother hit me like a gut punch. My mother, who had given everything for me, was kind, innocent, and undeserving of such a fate. I struggled to push the crushing weight of it all from my mind.

When I finally snapped out of it, Peter and Luna stared at me. I must have spaced out longer than I realised. Luna asked, furrowing her brow in concern, "Are you okay?"

I forced a nod, my voice unconvincing. Peter added, "We'll figure this out, Gwen. We just need a plan, a solid plan."

I wanted to believe him, but what could we realistically do? Peter was right: we wouldn't make it to Los Angeles in time. Zeus was going to kill my mother. We had no idea what happened after the attack or who helped us. It all felt hopeless.

We tried to piece together what we remembered. Unfortunately, we were all on the same page, attacked by the Furies; Luna's lightning shield shattered, a horn sounded, horses galloped, and arrows rained down. And then everything went black.

Peter broke the silence with sarcasm. "Well, that's a lot to go on."

"I know it's not ideal, but it's not like we can do much about it," Luna snapped.

I was about to lash out, but I stopped myself. "Will you two stop? This isn't helping. What happened before doesn't matter. What matters now is what we do going forward."

They both fell silent and nodded.

"Right. So, what now?" I asked, my voice more determined this time.

Luna and Peter exchanged a glance. Then Luna sighed. "We don't know, Gwen. We're out of ideas. We don't even know where we are or who brought us here."

I paused, and then it hit me: the map Hermes had given us. "What about the map? It should help us find our way."

Luna's face fell. "I'm sorry, Gwen, but the map was destroyed in the blast from the bus. It's gone."

Those words echoed in my head. The map was gone. My stomach dropped. "So that's it," I said softly, almost to myself. "We're finished. My mother's going to die, and it's all my fault. The map was supposed to lead us to the Palace of Death, and now it's gone."

I could see Luna's hand reaching out to comfort me, but before she could, a rustling sound came from the trees behind us. Peter quickly motioned for us to hide.

We dove behind a large rock, Peter gripping his spear, ready for whatever or whoever was approaching. A familiar figure emerged from the trees: a black horse's body, black hair, and light blue eyes. There was no mistaking who it was.

"Chiron!" Luna shouted.

We rushed to him, throwing our arms around him in relief.

He smiled and laughed; his voice warm. "Gwen, Luna, Peter... I'm so glad you're all alright. When I saw the Furies attack, I feared I was too late."

I wiped tears from my eyes. "So, it was you who saved us?"

Chiron smiled. "Yes, my child. I'm happy I got to you in time."

Peter, still cautious, asked, "But how did you know we needed help?"

Chiron's smile widened. "I grew worried about you all on this quest. So, I sought the Oracle. She told me the prophecy that Olympus's deadliest beings attacked you. I knew I had to act fast, so I ran here quickly. Centaurs can cover incredible distances in no time."

As he spoke, a plan began to form in my mind. But Luna asked what we were all thinking. "Do you know where we are, Chiron?"

His smile softened. "Yes, you're about half an hour away from where the bus exploded. I thought it best to set up camp here, so you could rest and heal with Ambrosia."

Chiron had gone out of his way for us. Not many would risk so much for the daughter of a Titan. I knew he understood, after all; he was also a child of Cronus. Maybe that was why he cared.

After explaining, Chiron offered us breakfast of eggs, bacon, and lemonade. And let me tell you, he could cook. The bacon was crispy, and the eggs were perfectly cooked. We devoured it gratefully, but Chiron smiled and said, "No need to thank me. I'm the protector of all Half-Bloods."

Once we finished, I turned to him, the weight of everything pressing down on me. "I've failed."

Chiron's eyes widened with concern. "What do you mean, Gwen?"

"I couldn't save my mother. We won't make it to the Underworld in time. The map Hermes gave us was destroyed, and now Hades is going to kill her. It's all my fault."

Chiron let me finish, his gaze soft. When I stopped, he spoke in a calm, sympathetic tone. "Gwen, you have not failed. No Half-Blood has faced what you've endured. The fact that you've come this far without real help is incredible. You've surprised me, and you will make it in time."

I looked at him, confused. "How?"

He smiled. "I'm going to give you all a lift. You'll ride with me."

The words didn't sink in at first. "What do you mean?" Luna asked.

Chiron's grin widened. "You remember how fast centaurs can run? I'll carry you to California. After that, you'll have to find the Palace of Death on your own. I'm sorry, but I can't do more."

We all stared at him for a moment, stunned. Then, I couldn't help it; I grinned. "Thank you, Chiron. Thank you so much."

Chiron's smile never wavered. "Think nothing of it. Just consider it a favor for someone who wants to see you succeed."

He knelt, and we climbed onto his back, holding on tight. "Ready?" he asked.

We nodded, and with that, he sped off toward California. The wind rushed past us, and I felt hope for the first time in a long while. I was going to save my mother; I had to.

WE FINALLY REACH LOS ANGELES

Chiron wasn't kidding when he said centaurs could run fast. We sped past fields, deserted country roads, forests, and mountains. It felt like the world around us blurred into streaks of green and brown. The wind whipped through my hair, stinging my face like I was on the fastest roller coaster. The thrill surged through me, a rush of excitement and dopamine. I clung to Chiron's back, barely able to keep up with the force of his speed.

Luna's voice broke through the wind. "Look there!"

I barely caught a glimpse of a sign. "Welcome to Utah," it read. My heart skipped a beat. We were really on our way.

Chiron glanced over his shoulder; his expression filled with amusement. "Ah, Utah. Would you kids like to pass King's Peak and Salt Lake City? It'll be a nice detour before we reach the Nevada deserts."

We all exchanged a look, still racing against time but at a pace where every minute felt like an eternity. Taking the detour wouldn't make much of a difference. We nodded in agreement, and Chiron grinned, speeding toward King's Peak.

The world zipped by us, and I couldn't believe that no one on the roads seemed to notice we were riding a mythical creature. I suspected Hecate's magic was at work again, concealing the truth from the world. It made me wonder if my favorite author was secretly a Half-Blood too. But some secrets were meant to stay hidden.

The Green River appeared before us, winding its way toward the mountains. Chiron turned sharply and leaped into the river with a heavy splash. He skimmed across the surface, following the river's path, effortlessly gaining speed.

"Chiron, you can walk on water?" I gasped, unable to contain my amazement.

He laughed heartily. "Sure, I can. I have to go fast enough, but most of my kin can do the same."

We continued, following the river into a vast forest. The trees flashed by so quickly that it was like we were cutting through the very heart of the forest. Chiron dodged trees and obstacles so precisely that it almost felt like he wasn't even trying. It was a sight to behold, and it left me in awe.

Luna tapped me on the back. "See? I told you Chiron was amazing. Never doubt me again, Gwen."

I rolled my eyes but smiled. "Sure, shut up, tomboy." My nickname caught her off guard. I'd started calling her Thunderhead, and I could see the grin forming on her face. She liked the nicknames.

"It's nice to hear that nickname again, cowgirl. It reminds me of when we were just schoolgirls," Luna teased. "Even back then, I was always protecting you."

I didn't like the nickname, but hearing it again made me laugh. For a moment, it felt like things were back to normal. I wasn't running from gods or monsters. I was a normal girl living on a farm with my mom, the animals, and my two amazing horses. I hadn't thought about them in a while. I wondered if they had survived the attack on my farm.

We continued through the forest, the river leading us toward the mountains. Chiron suddenly motioned for us to look to our left. We stared for a long moment at twigs moving among the trees.

Peter broke the silence. "I know what they are. Those are tree nymphs. I knew they blended in well with the environment, but this is amazing."

Chiron smiled at him. "Peter's right. Those are tree nymphs. They usually keep to themselves in their little communities, but some help at the fort as doctors and nurses."

A thought struck me, and I asked, "Luna told me you usually have children of Apollo as doctors. Why the tree nymphs back at the fort when I was there?"

Chiron paused, considering my question. "You're correct, Gwen. We normally rely on the children of Apollo for this kind of work. But some Half-Bloods get injured just coming to the Fort, or when they leave. So, for those who can't make it back on their own we often send the children of Apollo on dangerous missions to help other Half-Bloods. While they're gone, we use tree nymphs as temporary replacements so the children of Apollo can help those in need."

It made sense. The children of Apollo must be incredibly brave and skilled to put themselves at risk every day. I didn't know if I had that kind of courage. My powers barely worked on a good day, and when they did, people often doubted me.

We climbed higher into the mountains, the towering King's Peak looming ahead. At 13,533 feet, it stood above us like a silent sentinel. Chiron's grin widened. "We're going to the top. Hold on tight."

We tightened our grip as he leapt into the air, using his bow and magic to ascend quickly. At the top, we could see the clouds beneath us and Salt Lake City in the distance. The cold wind sliced through the air, stinging my face. For a moment, it felt like I was soaring through the sky.

Without warning, Chiron leapt down the mountain, and the world blurred as we screamed in exhilaration. It was like the best roller coaster ride I'd ever experienced. The rush was intoxicating. When the thrill finally subsided, we zipped through Salt Lake City, passing tall buildings, cars, and buses before leaping across the Great Salt Lake. I could see the fish darting beneath the water, scattering in every direction.

As we neared the Nevada border, Chiron's voice turned serious. "We're entering northern Nevada. The desert's ahead, and it's treacherous. Many creatures, mythical and otherwise, roam here. I'll stay cautious, but you three need to cover me if anything attacks."

We nodded, bracing ourselves. Chiron slowed his pace slightly as the rocky desert stretched out before us. The heat was suffocating, the sun beating down relentlessly. Luna looked over at Chiron. "Wouldn't it be faster to just speed across straight into California?"

Chiron's face grew tense. "Some of the creatures here are fast enough to catch me if I'm speeding. I won't have time to react if something attacks me."

The desert was brutally hot, and the oppressive silence weighed on us. But then, in the distance, something moved. Chiron stiffened, his senses alert. "Prepare yourselves," he said, his voice sharp.

As the figures drew closer, I could see them clearly. "Other centaurs," Peter breathed in awe.

They raced past us, their speed almost matching Chiron's. Chiron watched them pass, tears welling in his eyes. "It's been a long time since I've met anyone of my kind," he murmured, his voice thick with emotion. "I was the first of my kind, the only one descended from Cronus. I wish I could ride with them, but... my connection to the Titan Lord means I'm not welcome."

I understood how Chiron felt. Sometimes, it felt like I didn't belong either. But Chiron wiped his tears away, his smile returning. "Enough of that. Let's keep going."

We picked up speed again, but still cautiously, watching for any monsters. Fortunately, we made it through Nevada without encountering any dangers. The desert gave way to the outskirts of California, and I felt a wave of relief. This was it. We were getting closer to my mother.

As we approached Los Angeles, Chiron slowed, and we reached the outskirts of the city. "This is where we part ways," he said, his voice serious. "Good luck, little ones. I hope you've got a plan for dealing with Hades."

We thanked him, and Chiron sped off into the distance. Luna turned to us, her eyes focused. "This is it. Be ready."

We nodded in silent agreement, our hearts racing as we entered Los Angeles. The search for the Palace of Death and the Underworld entrance was about to begin.

THE ENTRANCE TO THE DARK ONE'S REALM

As we walked through the crowded streets of Los Angeles, the city felt lively and overwhelming. The sun's warmth, towering buildings, and casinos lining the streets all made it seem like the city of dreams until we remembered our fundamental mission: to find the Palace of Death. However without the map Hermes had given us, we were utterly lost.

Luna broke the silence. "OK, how about we ask someone for directions?"

Peter raised an eyebrow, his voice laced with doubt. "Luna, are you sure that's a good idea? We're three random kids in the middle of LA, searching for a hotel called the Palace of Death. People aren't going to take us seriously."

I nodded in agreement but offered a possible solution. "What if we tell them we're meeting family there? Our parents must have given us directions." I said, but then my tone shifted as I began considered it more carefully. "No, if that were true, they would have told us exactly how to get there. People would see right through that."

Peter's expression darkened. However despite his expression Luna didn't back down. "Then we'll just tell a police officer that we got lost after grabbing ice cream. It's a simple story, and they're more likely to help us."

Peter hesitated, clearly concerned. "Are you sure about this plan, Luna?"

Luna met his gaze with determination. "We don't have much of a choice, Peter. Without Hermes's map, we need to make it work."

Peter seemed to swallow his doubts but didn't argue further. Luna smiled, triumphant. "Good, then it's settled."

I glanced at both of them. "Great, but how do we find a police officer in this giant city?"

Peter shrugged. "I guess we just walk down this street and hope for the best. We'll run into one eventually."

We all agreed, and so we began our walk. Los Angeles lived up to its reputation. The sun shone brightly, a light breeze swept through the streets, and the towering buildings seemed endless. The city was a place of contrasts, beautiful yet chaotic, peaceful yet full of temptation, especially with the glimmering casinos everywhere. It was easy to see why they called it the City of Fallen Angels.

After half an hour of walking, we decided to take a break at a local coffee shop. Inside, we ordered three lattes from a young barista and settled into a corner by the window, sipping our drinks as we pondered our next move. We had to find a police officer, and quickly.

I turned to Luna, a question lingering in my mind. "Luna, be honest with me. How dangerous is the Underworld?"

Luna took a slow sip of her coffee before answering calmly and thoughtfully. "It's extremely dangerous, Gwen. Most people never make it out alive. The Underworld is home to monsters and dark forces, and as we discussed before, it's split into three realms. First, there's Tartarus, where the Titans, including your father Cronus, are imprisoned. Then, there's Elysium, a paradise for the heroic and virtuous, where they live in eternal peace. But we don't need to worry about those places. We should focus on the realm that leads to Hades's castle."

I understood the gravity of her words. "The Fields of Asphodel."

Luna nodded. "Yes, Gwen. The Fields of Asphodel are where souls linger without judgment. It's at the edge of those fields where Hades's castle lies. That's where your mother is being held, locked away by

Hades on Zeus's orders. We need to focus on getting through Asphodel."

I paused, thinking about the monsters we might encounter. "How many monsters should we expect in Asphodel?"

Luna glanced down at her cup, taking a moment to consider her answer. "Well Gwen. Most souls in Asphodel are content to live in peace. The main threat is Cerberus, the three-headed hound of Hell. He devours the truly evil before they can be judged. Aside from that, you'll encounter a few minor gods, some primordial gods, and of course, Hades, Persephone, their son Zagreus the God of rebirth he helps souls who choose to be reborn instead of Elysium, and their daughter Melinoe the Goddess of Nightmares and Ghosts, who punishes the souls in Tartarus. But the real danger lies in Cerberus."

Her words calmed me somewhat. At least the odds weren't as bad as I'd feared. But there was still much to worry about. "And the primordial gods? Which ones are we likely to encounter?"

Luna thought for a moment before replying. "Thanatos, the primordial god of death, is the main one. He's the son of Nyx, the goddess of night. Nyx sometimes visits him, but she doesn't stay in the Underworld. Erebus, the primordial god of darkness, is Nyx's husband, but he hasn't been seen in centuries. So it's mainly Nyx and Thanatos we might run into."

I processed all this information, but something still nagged at me. "So, we'll be fine getting to Hades's castle?"

Peter snorted, his sarcasm cutting through the tension. "Oh, sure, getting there will be easy. Just walk up and knock on the door. It's getting out of the Underworld that's the real problem."

I froze, realizing the truth in his words. Once we get my mother safe, we can't just walk out. Hades wouldn't let us leave without a fight. He could summon monsters from all the realms to attack us if we tried to escape.

Suddenly, a wave of panic hit me. "Luna, the orb Hermes gave us, the one to help my mother get back, please tell me it's still intact."

Luna immediately checked it, her face relaxing with relief. "It's fine, Gwen. The orb is still in one piece."

I breathed a sigh of relief, but a familiar voice interrupted us before I could say anything more.

"I'm glad one thing I gave you is still intact."

We turned to see Hermes sitting beside me, his black hair and sandals unmistakable. His wings were hidden, but everything else was the same. He looked at us with a mix of regret and concern.

"I knew you were in trouble," he continued. "But I didn't think the Furies would come after you. Gwen, you've really angered Zeus. He wasn't happy that you survived the attack."

Peter was the first to speak, his voice skeptical. "If Zeus is that angry, why are you risking talking to us? Aren't you afraid of his wrath?"

Hermes chuckled softly. "I appreciate your concern, Peter, but I'm fine. I'm one of the twelve Olympians. Zeus won't punish me too harshly. But you two, Luna and Peter, you're both starting to look like enemies of Olympus. Helping Gwen is making Zeus very angry."

I glanced at Peter and Luna. For a brief moment, fear flickered in their eyes before they quickly masked it. Luna spoke up, her voice determined. "It doesn't matter. We won't abandon Gwen, no matter what."

Hermes gave a slight frown, his usual grin fading. "Of course. She's your friend, after all." He paused, then smiled again. "Now, how about I help you find the Palace of Death?"

We looked at him with grateful eyes, and Luna nodded eagerly. "Yes, please, Lord Hermes. We've been lost for a while now. If you can show us how to get to the Palace of Death, we would be eternally grateful."

Hermes gave us a slight nod. "Follow me. I'll take you there."

Without waiting for another word, he led us through the city. As we walked, he began to chat casually. "You know, being the god of travelers suits me. I love exploring. I used to protect adventurers who were setting off to find new lands."

I raised an eyebrow. "Used to?"

Hermes glanced back; his eyes filled with a hint of sadness. "Yes, Gwen. With every new continent discovered, there's less need for adventurers. No more lands to explore, no more people to protect."

We all felt sympathy for him, but Hermes's mood soon lifted. He turned a corner, and the Palace of Death stood before us.

"Here we are," Hermes said with a slight grin. "Glad to be of help."

Before we could express our appreciation, he disappeared without a trace. Standing before the ominous entrance to the Underworld, I felt a wave of anxiety wash over me, but also a deep sense of determination. I was about to face the unimaginable to save my mother.

"Let's go," Luna said, her voice steady. We took our first steps toward the entrance, fully aware that everything was about to change.

JOURNEY ACROSS THE UNDERWORLD

We pushed open the huge black wooden doors to the Palace of Death, stepping into the grand lobby. It was like something out of a high-budget movie: the purple carpet beneath our feet, the tall black pillars lining the walls, and the stained-glass windows overhead. The glass told stories, intricate images capturing the most famous tales of Greek mythology. One window depicted Heracles and his Twelve Labors, another showed Perseus battling Medusa, and in the next, Odysseus navigated the dangers after the Trojan War. I stood there, mesmerised by the vibrant colors and the stories they told, but the urgency of our mission pulled me back to reality.

Slowly, we moved toward the main desk, our footsteps echoing across the empty space. The desk was crafted from dark oak, its surface covered with rich red fabric. To the left, a small red button caught my eye. It read "Press for Service." I turned to Luna, a hesitant thought bubbling up inside me. "Do you want to do the honors?"

Luna's eyes widened, fear flickering in her gaze. "Gwen, remember—this is no ordinary hotel. It's a front, a disguise. We're standing at the entrance to the Underworld itself. And if you press that button, the Ferryman, Charon, will come."

Peter, ever the optimist, jumped in. "Isn't that what we need? We came here for him. We need Charon to enter the Underworld."

Luna hesitated, her brow furrowing as she took a deep breath. "I know," she said slowly turning to face me as she continued. "But we can't rush into this. The Underworld is full of dangers, Gwen. Worse still, we don't just need to save your mom. We need to find a way to get you out, too. Hades will expect you to stay." Her words hung in the air, and I couldn't shake the anxiety that bubbled up inside me.

I felt a tightness in my chest. I hated feeling like a burden, but there was no time for doubts. "Let me use my abilities. I can slow down and escape if things go wrong. I know you've said no before, but this might be our only chance."

Luna's face hardened, and her voice was firm as she cut me off. "No, Gwen. You can't control your powers. The Gods already want to imprison you because of what you are. You can't give them another reason to hate you." The words hit me harder than I expected, her distrust suffocating me.

I clenched my fists, fighting the growing sense of betrayal. My friends didn't trust me, not truly. The thought stung, but I pushed it aside. There was too much at stake.

I reached forward and pressed the red button. It buzzed loudly, Luna and Peter froze, staring at the desk in shock. Moments later, an old man appeared at the front desk. At first, he looked like a normal human, but when he spoke, his calm voice sent a chill down my spine. "Ah, Half-bloods, I see. No need for this mortal disguise, then." He snapped his fingers, and his appearance changed before our eyes.

His hair was as white as snow, his long beard flowing down to his chest. His skin was pale, veins glowing purple beneath the surface. His eyes, black and hollow, locked onto us with an unsettling intensity. He wore a long black cloak that swirled around him like smoke. "My name is Charon, but some people just call me Ferryman. What can I do for you, little Half-bloods?"

We were frozen in shock for a good while, just trying to process how quickly his appearance had changed. It wasn't until he spoke again that we snapped out of it. "Didn't that Centaur teach you it's rude to stare?"
I answered first, a hint of fear in my voice. "Sorry, sir, but do you mean Chiron when you say that Centaur?"

Charon's eyes flashed with annoyance, and he gritted his teeth. "Yes, I mean him. But never mention his name in my presence again."

I was ready to let it go, but Luna and Peter weren't. Their expressions darkened, and Luna spoke up with cold authority. "Do you have a problem with Chiron?"

Charon's lips curled into a sneer. "So, what if I do? He's just another self-righteous fool, thinking he's better than everyone else. Anyway, it's none of your business."

Peter couldn't hold his temper. He stepped forward, his fists clenched, his voice rising in anger. "How dare you speak about him like that? Chiron has been like a father to many of us, cared for us when no one else would!"

Luna's voice cut through the tension, sharp with concern. "Peter, please. He's a deity, remember? You don't want to anger him." Her tone softened as she added, "We're all on edge, but let's not make things worse."

Peter paused, his anger giving way to guilt. He lowered his head and let out a long sigh. "I'm sorry, sir. I shouldn't have let my emotions take control."

Charon studied him for a moment before speaking, his voice calmer now. "Apology accepted. I appreciate the work Chiron does for Half-bloods, but I'm not him. Humans mix us up all the time, and I get tired of it. He's liked, and I'm the dark, unapproachable one. It gets old. You could call it pettiness, if you like."

A flicker of understanding crossed my mind. He wasn't just a terrifying figure; he was burdened by comparisons and constantly overshadowed by Chiron's better reputation. For the first time, I felt a twinge of sympathy for him despite his frightening appearance.

I spoke up, my voice firm but respectful. "Charon, we need to enter the Fields of Asphodel."

He frowned, suspicion crossing his features. "For what purpose? The Underworld isn't a place to visit lightly. Not many make it back."

I didn't flinch. "I'm expected at Lord Hades' castle on the far edge of the Fields."

Charon raised an eyebrow. "I wasn't informed of any such meeting. Why would Hades want to see you?"

Before Luna or Peter could stop me, I spoke, the words tumbling out in a mix of fear and determination. "I'm Gwen Sallow. I'm a Half-blood. My father is Cronus, the Titan Lord. Hades has my mother."

The room went deathly silent. Luna and Peter looked at me, their eyes wide with shock and disbelief.

After what felt like an eternity, Charon spoke, his voice thick with surprise. "I didn't know... This changes things. I'll take you to the Fields of Asphodel, but I can't make exceptions. You'll need to pay the fare."

Luna nodded, her face tense. "How much?"

"Ten Drachmas each," Charon said after a moment's thought. "Do you have that?"

We quickly counted out thirty Drachmas and handed them over. Charon took the money and motioned for us to follow him. He led us to a small iron door at the back of the lobby. With a key from his pocket, he unlocked it and opened it, revealing a pitch–black room. The only light came from a small lantern on a wooden boat waiting inside.

"Step carefully," Charon said, his tone more serious now. "And keep your bodies inside the boat at all times."

We did as instructed, but the boat creaked under our weight. Charon snapped his fingers, and suddenly, the ship lifted into the air, my stomach dropping with weightlessness. Below us, the Underworld stretched out, dark, eerie, and cold. The fields were shrouded in thick fog, and dark trees were like silent sentinels. Hooded figures moved in the distance, their faces hidden, lost to the world.

We descended slowly, the oppressive atmosphere growing heavier the closer we reached the ground. Charon landed the boat with a jolt, his cold gaze fixed on me. "I'll be here when you return. Though... not all of you may come back."

His words cut through me like ice, and I couldn't shake the feeling that his gaze held more meaning than he let on.

We stepped off the boat and into the misty Fields of Asphodel. The air was thick with a sense of foreboding. I tried speaking to some hooded figures, but they didn't respond, their faces vacant and blank.

Luna's hand tightened on my shoulder. "Don't," she warned softly. "They don't know where they are, not until they're judged."

"Judged?" I asked, my curiosity piqued.

Luna looked around nervously. "It could take centuries, but they'll never know."

We pressed on, the fog thickening around us. As we walked, I noticed a fiery portal to our left, the very one I had seen in my dreams. The voice echoed once more, a familiar command. "Run."

I spoke back, my heart pounding. "I can't. I must save my mother. Who are you?"

There was a pause, as if the voice was weighing my words. Then, it spoke again, softer now, almost like it was trying to comfort me.

"Look down."

Confused, I blinked and glanced at the ground. My eyes landed on a small orange gemstone, glowing faintly against the mist.

"Use that when you're in trouble," the voice urged. "Say 'help me' into the gemstone, and it will take you somewhere safe. Please."

I reached down and picked up the gemstone, my thoughts racing with questions. However before I could ask anything more, the voice vanished, replaced by Luna's voice calling out to me. She was looking at me with concern etched on her face. "Gwen, are you okay?"

"I'm fine," I replied quickly, hiding the gemstone in my pocket.

We continued walking, the weight of the Underworld pressing down on us. Until a bright light appeared in the distance. "Elysium," Peter breathed, awe in his voice.

Luna nodded, but her expression was troubled. "It's beautiful, but we can't stop. Hades' castle is still ahead."

The fog grew thicker, making it harder to see. Peter's frustration broke through. "We'll never get anywhere in this fog. It's too thick!"

Luna sighed. "What choice do we have? We have to keep moving."

Peter stopped in his tracks. "We could be going in circles. We need to think, Luna."

After a long moment, Luna agreed, and we paused to regroup. I thought for a moment looking at the trees, then I turned to Luna. "Your lightning bolts, can they catch fire? Like, to light something?"

Luna's eyes lit up with understanding. "If the wood is dry enough, yes."

We found a dry branch, and, with careful aim, Luna struck it with a lightning bolt. The branch erupted into flames, casting light through the fog.

With renewed resolve, we moved forward, the castle looming ahead. Its towering black walls and gemstone pillars sparkled in the flickering light. We were close, so close.

Luna grabbed my shoulder, her voice low. "This is it. This is what we've been fighting for. Are you ready?"

I nodded, my heart pounding in my chest. "I'm coming, Mom. I'll save you."

We moved toward the castle, ready to face whatever awaited us inside.

THE BETRAYAL

We approached the massive doors at the castle's entrance. If the gemstone-covered pillars had been beautiful, the door was a work of pure extravagance. It gleamed with a golden sheen, and diamonds scattered across it gave it an almost ethereal sparkle. I stared at it in awe, its magnificence taking my breath away.

Peter was the first to speak, his voice full of admiration and confusion. "This castle is stunning, but how do we get inside? Do we just knock?"

I paused, considering our next move. "I guess we just knock," I said, though I had no idea what would answer the door. That was the real question.

Luna stayed silent, lost in thought. I could see the unease in her expression. Like me, she had no idea what might be on the other side of that door. A monster? A servant? Or something far worse? The uncertainty gnawed at me, but we had come this far.

I reached out to knock, but before I could, Luna's hand grabbed my shoulder. "Gwen," she said, her voice soft with concern, "we don't know who or what will open that door. Maybe we should find another way."

She had a point. But I was too far in to back out now. I looked her in the eyes, my voice firm. "I'm sorry, Luna. This is the way. We've come this far. Might as well get it over with."

Before she could stop me again, I knocked three times. The sound echoed, deep and resounding, like it came from the very heart of the Underworld.

Peter shifted nervously beside me. "Well, there's no turning back now. Whatever happens, happens. Keep your guard up."

We stood there for several long minutes, waiting. Every passing second stretched out with dread. Then, the sound of deliberate footsteps reached us—slow, calculated, almost as if they wanted us to hear them coming. Tension shot through the group as we braced for whatever would come.

We heard the unmistakable sound of locks turning, massive, heavy locks that sounded like something straight out of a bank vault. The golden door creaked open, and two figures emerged from the shadows. We all froze, staring in disbelief.

"Victoria and Amanda," I said, my voice tinged with annoyance and surprise. "Not you two again."

Luna mirrored my frustration. "Haven't we had enough of you already?"

The two women stood there, grinning, their expressions coldly amused. Victoria stepped forward, her smile widening as she spoke. "My, my, little Half-Blood. Is that any way to greet an old friend?" She let out a soft, wicked laugh.

I snapped back at her, my anger rising. "Old friend? Don't make me laugh. You're just a sinister witch I'd rather never see again."

Victoria showed no anger, but I caught the twitch in her face. I'd struck a nerve.

"How interesting," she replied, her voice smooth, though her eyes gleamed with something darker. "I'm surprised you survived the Furies' attack. Very surprised. But I imagine you'd have died if that Centaur hadn't gotten involved. Lucky you."

Peter and Luna stiffened at the mention of Chiron; their anger evident. But neither of them spoke, unwilling to provoke a fight in Hades' domain.

Amanda, ever the calm one, smiled widely. "As much as I'd love to chat more, we really shouldn't keep His Majesty waiting. Lord Hades expects us."

Victoria sighed, regaining some composure. "Yes, yes, you're right. We mustn't keep Lord Hades waiting." She turned back to us. "If you'd like, we can guide you to the throne room."

We hesitated. Every encounter with these two had ended in betrayal, manipulation, or worse. We couldn't trust them, but what choice did we have? We didn't know the layout of this castle, and they likely had more knowledge of it than we did. Reluctantly, we nodded, agreeing to follow them.

"Very good," Amanda said, her voice dripping with mock sweetness. "Half-Bloods really can be cooperative when given the right incentive."

Victoria smiled in agreement. But I could see the bitterness in Peter's eyes and the frustration in Luna's. None of us were happy to be trusting these women, but it was the only option.

Inside the castle, the opulence was overwhelming. The walls, black as night, shimmered with embedded gemstones, casting colorful glimmers around us. The floor was made of Rainbow Quartz, and the windows were crafted from pure Amethyst. Pearls hung from the ceiling, glowing with an otherworldly white light.

"This place is beautiful," I murmured, almost in awe.

Amanda chuckled. "Did you expect anything less from the God of Wealth?"

I frowned. "I thought Hades was the God of the Underworld."

Victoria smirked slightly, but Amanda answered. "Hades is the King of the Underworld, yes, but there's no 'God of the Underworld.' It's simply the title of King, and Hades holds that title."

"So, he's the king of the Underworld but has the title of God of Wealth?" I asked, still confused.

"Exactly," Amanda said, smiling as if talking to a child.

They led us through countless rooms—dining halls, living rooms, and bedrooms—each one more magnificent than the last. But with every step, the sense of dread grew heavier. How long until we reached the throne room? What would happen when we did?

Luna's impatience finally broke through. "How much longer until we reach the throne room?"

Victoria's tone was calm but sharp. "Not far now. I just thought we'd give you a little scenic tour. Not every day Half-Bloods get to see a place like this. Are you not grateful?"

Luna's voice was thick with defiance. "We're here to save Gwen's mother. That's the only reason we're rushing."

Victoria laughed. "Yes, yes, I know all about that. I was the one who took her, you know, by order of Lord Zeus and Lord Hades."

At her words, fury surged through me. "It was you!" I shouted, unable to keep my voice steady.

"Yes," Victoria replied, her smile twisted. "After I recovered from Luna's lightning bolt, Zeus and Hades sent me to kidnap your mother. I saw you fight the Minotaur. You were impressive, Gwen, but I took your mother without you even noticing."

My anger flared to an unbearable level. "My mother was innocent! But you don't care about that, do you? You just follow orders, like the loyal pet you are."

Luna shouted at me, "Gwen, calm down! Getting angry won't help us!"

But I couldn't stop. "You're really going to side with her? She's the reason my mother's trapped with Hades!"

Luna hugged me, trying to calm me down. "I know, I know," she whispered. "But we need to focus on getting your mother out, not making things worse."

With great effort, I took a deep breath, trying to reign in my anger. Luna was right. We had to think carefully.

Finally, I looked at Victoria, my voice cold. "Take us to the throne room. Take us to Hades."

Victoria sneered. "Very well. No more detours."

We walked for a few more minutes before arriving at a door made of pure sapphire. Amanda opened it with a flourish. "This is the throne room. Lord Hades awaits."

We stepped inside, and the sight before us was breathtaking. The floor was made of pure diamond, and pillars of ruby supported the towering ceiling. Lord Hades sat in the center on an obsidian throne.

We stopped a few feet away from him. His presence was overwhelming. His skin was pale, almost ghostly, and his golden eyes glowed with an intensity that made my heart race. He wore a black cloak lined with gold, the fabric catching the light as he looked us over.

After a moment of tense silence, Lord Hades spoke in a voice unnervingly similar to Zeus'. "I know who you Half-Bloods are," he said, his gaze shifting to Luna on my left. "Luna Williams, daughter of Zeus." He turned to my right and added, "Peter Winter, son of Athena." His eyes lingered on me longer than the others, a hint of recognition crossing his face. "Ah, the Titan's spawn. Well, it's nice to meet you at last, my dear little sister."

I stepped forward, defiance flaring in my chest. Luna tried to hold me back, but I shrugged off her grip. "Release my mother, now Dark one," I said, my voice thick with anger. "She doesn't deserve this."

Hades looked at me, his face a mask of shock and fury. "What did you call me?" he hissed. "Dark One? Where did you get that name for me, girl?"

I met his gaze with unwavering defiance, my tone still sharp with rage. "It suits you," I said, not backing down." Plus the Oracle told me, I shall go West and find the doors to the Dark One's realm."

His eyes narrowed. "I've been called many things, but never the Dark One. I am far kinder than my siblings."

"If that's true," I snapped, "then why did you take my mother? She's innocent!"

Luna's voice cut through. "Gwen, please, stop."

But I wasn't listening. "Give her back, Hades."

Hades waved his hand at that, and my mother appeared before me. She was handcuffed but unharmed. When she saw me, tears welled in her eyes. "Gwen, no! You shouldn't have come back for me."

"Mom," I cried, my heart breaking.

Hades spoke coldly. "She'll be released only when you surrender to me."

Peter and Luna summoned their weapons, Luna's voice cutting through the air. "Like hell she's surrendering to you!" But before they could make a move, Hades raised his hand, his magic chaining them to the floor. He laughed, a dark, echoing sound. "So now you care? You've spent this entire time judging her powers because she's the daughter of Cronus. You may not have meant to, but that's how it came across to her. And it's how you felt deep down. Am I wrong?"

I glanced back at them, secretly hoping they would tell me it wasn't true, that the things I had been feeling were wrong.

After a long silence, Luna spoke up, her voice softer than I'd ever heard it. "We're sorry, Gwen. I guess we've secretly been judging you. We were wrong too, and we are sorry. But Lord Hades, she is not evil. She is not like Cronus."

"And yet," Hades interrupted with a grin, "she's been secretly talking to him, and you didn't even realise it."

"What?" Luna said, shock and confusion in her voice.

Hades continued, his eyes glinting with amusement. "The voice she's been hearing in her sleep, she started hearing it in the real world too. She's been talking to Cronus."

Luna's eyes widened as she turned to me. "Gwen, is that true?"

Without hesitation, I nodded. "I didn't know it was Cronus. But yes, I've been talking to him. I didn't tell you because I didn't think I could trust you because of how much you were judging me because of my powers."

Luna lowered her head, guilt clearly eating at her. The chains around her wrists seemed to dig in harder as she fought against them. Hades spoke again, his tone colder now. "Now then, Gwen Sallow, are you going to obey the deal?"

My mother screamed; her voice frantic. "Gwen, don't you dare! Don't listen to him! Don't do this!"

I looked at my mother, torn between anger and a deep sadness. I wanted to save her but couldn't let her stay here. I had no choice. "I'm sorry, Mom. I can't let you stay here. I agree, Lord Hades."

With a snap of his fingers, my mother was released. She rushed into my arms, her voice shaking as she begged me not to go through with it. I pulled out Hermes's orb and placed it gently in her hands. "Think of home. You'll be safe there I'll be ok mom."

She hesitated for a moment before nodding, and with a heavy heart, I threw the orb to the ground. My mother disappeared, back to the farm where she would be safe.

Hades stared at me, confusion flickering in his eyes. "What was that?"

I spoke softly, the weight of my actions pressing down on me. "The orb Hermes gave me. My mother should be back at the farm right now."

Hades looked even more puzzled. "But you just told her to think of home. Also you told her You'll be okay?"

I smiled faintly, relief washing over me. "I lied. It was the only way I could get her to go home safely."

"I see," Hades said, his voice darkening. "And now, you're my prisoner, Gwen Sallow."

I stood tall, my eyes glowing orange with power. "I'm afraid not, Lord Hades. I'm not staying here with you. I'm leaving, even if I have to use my powers to escape."

Luna shouted, desperation in her voice. "Wait, Gwen! If you use your powers now, you'll just make all of Olympus angrier. Let us speak to Chiron. Maybe he can figure out another way."

I turned to her, anger boiling over. "So, you would make me a prisoner of Hades?"

Luna tried to defend herself, her voice pleading. "Gwen, I know you're angry, and that's not what I meant."

I raised my hand, my fury exploding. "Silence!" I screamed, my body radiating orange light. Hades turned to his guards, his expression shifting to one of fury.

"Arrest her!" he ordered.

Victoria and Amanda lunged, but I slowed time, freezing everyone in place, including Luna, Peter, and Hades. Without a thought, I summoned Times Reaper. slashing through the guards effortlessly, the air humming with energy as I made my way toward the castle exit.

As I ran, I gave Luna and Peter one last look, my voice cold and bitter. "I'm done trusting you."

I sprinted through the castle halls, fighting off any monsters that crossed my path. The castle doors were within reach when I heard Hades call out, commanding his monsters to chase after me.

The ground shook as a skeletal army, swords drawn, along with Gorgons and Minotaurs, charged toward me. But I wasn't afraid. The fire in my chest, the burning rage, pushed me forward. I fought with everything I had. Every slash of Times Reaper, every battle cry from the monsters, only fueled my anger. I couldn't stop. I wouldn't stop.

Eventually, I found myself in the foggy forest of Asphodel, hiding behind trees, ambushing monsters one by one. Time was my ally now, and I bent it to my will as I cut down the enemies chasing me. After what seemed like hours, I arrived at the portal to Tartarus, the monsters hot on my heels.

I gripped Times Reaper tightly, preparing for another brutal fight. But just as the monsters closed in on me, I heard my father's voice again, clearer than ever. "Gwen, the gem."

Without a second thought, I pulled the orange gemstone from my pocket and whispered, "Take me somewhere safe."

In an instant, I was enveloped in an orange glow and teleported to the outskirts of my old farm. I looked around, the sight of my broken home filling me with a strange calm. But then, the sadness hit. I knew I couldn't stay here. My mother was safe, but I would have to leave forever.

I put the gem back in my pocket and my weapon returned to my necklace as I started walking toward my old home, knowing I had to say goodbye.

THE TEARFUL GOODBYE

I slowly made my way toward the farm, approaching the outskirts. The battered sign, "Welcome to Moonlight Valley Farm," barely stood. The fences were torn apart, and parts lay on the ground, destroyed by the Minotaur's attack. A lump formed in my throat as I took in the sight. The destruction of my family's home weighed on me. It was all because of who I was and who I was related to. I knew, deep down, that I couldn't stay here. The Olympians would continue to come after me. As long as I existed, I would be a danger to my mother and everything I loved. I couldn't trust anyone anymore. Luna and Peter had betrayed me, and that was a painful truth I had to accept. They showed me that no matter what I tried, I would always be viewed with fear and hatred.

But despite all that, I needed to say goodbye to my mother, at least one last time.

As I walked past the broken fences, my heart grew heavier with each step. Guilt gripped my soul. The sight of my old home in ruins overwhelmed me. Tears streamed down my face as I walked, trying to process everything. I saw a few of my sheep, chickens, and pigs scattered around. The animals didn't come to me, but they recognised me. The animals roamed freely, grazing on the grass in the fields and the forest, though they were not in need of food. They were the only things that still seemed to be okay.

Then, as I approached the remains of our family home, I saw her standing where the front door used to be my mother.

My heart ached at the sight of her. She had been through so much. My steps grew slower. I didn't know what I would say to her. I knew she wouldn't want me to leave, but I couldn't stay. If I did, she would be in danger.

Her back was turned, and I could see she was crying. My chest tightened. I stepped forward, unsure, but the word slipped from my lips.

"Mom."

She turned, shock flashing in her eyes before they softened with sadness. She rushed toward me, arms stretched wide, and hugged me tightly. She sobbed on my shoulder, calling my name over and over. I held her, unsure of what to say, my tears mixing with hers. She finally pulled away, her voice shaky as she whispered, "Gwen, I can't believe it. You're safe. But how did you get out? How did you escape Hades?"

I paused, then answered softly, "For a long time, I fought off monsters, freezing everything in my path. It lead me back to a portal leading to Tartarus. That's when Father spoke to me. He's been speaking to me in dreams, and in whispers. I didn't know it was him until. He gave me an orange gemstone that brought me here."

She took a deep breath, slowly releasing me from her hug. "Oh, he did? I'm so glad he's helping you."

But my heart was heavy as I looked at her, a hint of anger rising within me. "Did you know, Mom? Did you know my father was Cronus, King of the Titans?"

Her eyes widened, and she sat on the ground, her gaze dropping. "Yes," she whispered, her voice heavy with regret. "Your grandfather was the first to know. He told me when I was pregnant with you."

I sat beside her, waiting for her to continue.

My mother sighed, her hands trembling slightly. Years ago, your father found a way to escape Tartarus. He went on the run for about three years before I met him. At first, he didn't tell me who he was; he went by Jacob. But over time, I fell head over heels for him, and he fell deeply in love with me. I introduced him to your grandfather, who approved of us and he helped work on our farm for a long time. Then, when I got pregnant with you, your father finally revealed who he was. He told your grandfather first because your grandfather was also a Half-Blood."

"WHAT?" I said in complete shock. "Grandpa was a Half-Blood?"

My mother nodded, then continued, "Yes, Gwen. He was a Half-Blood, the son of Poseidon."

When she said that, everything clicked. I thought back to when I was being told which Olympians were on my side: Artemis, Athena, and Poseidon. It made no sense to me at the time why Poseidon would support me, but it made sense now. He's my great-grandfather.

I told my mother to continue, and she nodded. "Your grandfather agreed to keep it a secret, but by that point, it was too late. The whole of Olympus had already found out your father was really Cronus. Zeus came to take him away. Your father told your grandfather to take me inside and hide, and then a huge battle raged on between him and Zeus. I couldn't take it. I rushed outside and saw Zeus with his hand around your father's neck. The burn mark on the side of our house was from one of Zeus's lightning bolts. I ran up to Zeus and begged him to spare him because I was pregnant, but that only infuriated Zeus. He knew about the prophecy. That's when your father said he would go willingly back to Tartarus if Zeus would only spare me and our family.

Zeus agreed, but with a condition: you would never know who you were, and your powers would slowly fade away."

My mother's voice grew quieter. "That's why I tried to push you away from Hellenism. I tried so desperately to keep you hidden, to protect you. Your grandfather tried to do the same. However he knew you would eventually find out, he knew that we couldn't stop it. And you did. You found out."

I listened, trying to absorb everything. It hurt to hear how much my father, grandfather, and mother had suffered because of me. My mother looked around for a moment, then asked, "Where's Luna? And the boy you were with? Did they escape with you?"

I looked away, bitterness and tears streaming down my face. "I don't care, Mom. They betrayed me."

My mother looked shocked and saddened. "Honey, I'm sure that's not true. It must've been a misunderstanding. I know Luna, especially, would never—"

"MOM!" I snapped, my voice trembling with sadness and frustration. "Luna and the boy you saw me with, Peter, betrayed me. They were always afraid and skeptical of my powers because they were the powers of Cronus. When I freed you, they suggested I stay behind while they went to talk to Chiron about how to free me. They betrayed me, Mom. I can't trust anyone anymore."

My mother's face fell, deep sadness in her eyes, not knowing what to say. She just pulled me into a long hug. We stayed like that for a while before she said, "It doesn't matter, Gwen. We'll rebuild. We'll fix the house, the farm, everything. It'll be okay. I even found Bucephalus and Amphitrite." She whistled, and the two horses came running towards me, instantly recognizing me. I hugged them tightly, feeling their warmth, and for a moment, I wanted to stay in that beginning forever. But I knew I couldn't. I had to leave.

After a long while, I pulled away from the horses and from my mother, my heart heavy. I built up the courage to say what needed to be said. "I'm sorry, Mom."

She looked at me, confused. "What are you sorry for, honey?"

I closed my eyes, bracing myself. "I'm sorry, but I can't stay. Olympus will never stop sending people after me. As long as I'm here, you'll always be in danger. You'll never have a normal life. So, I'm sorry. But I'm leaving, and I don't intend to ever come back."

My mother's voice cracked, panic creeping in. "No, no, Gwen. Please, don't leave. We can fix this. You don't have to go. You don't have to run away."

She reached for me, but I stepped back, shaking my head. Her voice dropped to a whisper, full of desperation. "Gwen, please. Don't do this."

My heart shattered as I looked at her. I couldn't stay. If I did, she'd be in danger again. What if the Gods took her away? The trick wouldn't work a second time. "I'm sorry, Mom. But if I stay, I'll only put you in more danger. I can't risk it. But I needed to see you one last time before I left. I'm truly sorry."

I hugged Bucephalus and Amphitrite one last time before running towards the edge of the farm. My mother's desperate cries echoed behind me. "GWEN! GWEN, NO! PLEASE!"

She kept shouting, and each plea broke my heart even more. The pain inside me only deepened, but I couldn't turn back. I ran deeper into the forest, away from everything, until her cries faded. After a while, I stopped and rested against a tree, tears streaming down my face.

I thought about the prophecy. "You shall be looked at with fear and suspicion by those you love the most, and find yourself lost and alone when your story is complete." The more I thought about it, the more it made sense. "Fair play, Oracle," I whispered through my tears. "You were right. I thought that last part could never happen, but it has. I've been feared, and now I am lost and alone."

I let the tears fall, the lesson sinking in. Never again would I trust anyone fully.

About The Author

Dafydd Williams, born in Wales, has always been passionate about reading. He especially loves Rick Riordan's works, notably the Percy Jackson series. His childhood fascination with mythology and adventure sparked a deep desire to create his own stories. Inspired by Riordan's captivating blend of ancient myths and modern-day adventure, Dafydd is driven to write a book that captures the same sense of wonder and excitement, incorporating fantastical tales with relatable characters, just like his favourite author.

REFERENCES IN THIS BOOK

- Percy Jackson and the Olympians by Rick Riordan released June 28th, 2005.
- Edmund Randolph Wikipedia